Nature's Playthings

Also by Patrick Semple

A Parish Adult Education Handbook – Editor

Believe It Or Not – A Memoir

That Could Never Be – with K Dalton

The Rectory Dog – Poetry Collection

The Rector Who Wouldn't Pray For Rain – A Memoir

A Narrow Escape – Poetry Collection

Transient Beings – A Novel

Curious Cargo – A Travelogue

Being Published – A Creative Writing Guide

Slices of Life – A Collection of Short Stories

Nature's Playthings

Patrick Semple

Code Green Publishing

A catalogue record for this book is available from the British Library.

ISBN 978-1-907215-23-0

Version 1.0

Cover design by Code Green Publishing

Published by
Code Green Publishing
Coventry, England

www.codegreenpublishing.com

In Memoriam Jean Meslier

So nature deals with us, and takes away
Our playthings one by one, and by the hand
Leads us to rest so gently, that we go
Scarce knowing if we wish to go or stay,
Being too full of sleep to understand
How far the unknown transcends the what we know.

H.W. Longfellow

In nature there are neither rewards nor punishments;
there are consequences.

Robert Green Ingersoll

CHAPTER 1

I stood on the front step watching the removal men carrying the contents of my home into a van. I mused on the fact that many former rectors had stood on the same steps and watched strangers, who cared nothing for them, carry out their possessions and load them into a vehicle of some sort. This would surely emphasise for them, as it did for me, the transience of the life they lived and of the job they did. I was also conscious that I was almost certainly the only one in a long line of clergy of more than one hundred and fifty years who was moving because he no longer believed. Or was I? I felt that I was turning my back on the tradition that had sustained so many clergy and so many parishioners over the years. I had asked questions of myself but couldn't come up with answers that would allow me to stay. I couldn't work out why so many other people, clergy and lay, didn't seem to have the same kinds of question and if they did they must have found answers acceptable to them. On balance I believed that most people didn't ask the questions in the first place; they took everything on trust from clergy and teachers whom their parents had allowed to indoctrinate them as children, and whom they believed knew better than they did.

After Jennifer died the first thing I had to do was to pay off her debts. There were three people I knew to whom she had owed money: the grocer, the publican and one of her drinking companions. I started to put aside what spare cash I could before I decided I would talk to the bank manager, who had always been supportive of Jennifer and me. Having established that I would secure a job in the real world, he gave me a personal loan to pay off the three creditors immediately so that I would leave the parish financially in good standing.

This was more than could be said for my theological reputation. It had become known that the reason I was leaving the parish and the ministry was my loss of faith. This was a term I never used myself; 'loss of faith' sounded to me like culpable negligence which was far from the case. On the contrary; I arrived at this position after a long slow process of years of reading and of thought. Finally I found that I could no longer believe the basic doctrines of the Christian Church, which created tensions within me as I tried to perform my duty as a country rector. I had to be true to myself and wanted parishioners to think for themselves but did not necessarily want them to end up where I had. I had no desire whatever to convert people to my point of view. In fact I still had a great respect for people with a strong simple faith, but I was puzzled by people including, or perhaps particularly, clergy, many of whom had better minds than mine who either rationalised away any doubt they had, some of them by using all of what I considered the devious devices of modern theology, or else didn't bother to think at all about the issues that had become incredible to me.

Shortly after Jennifer died I gave notice to the bishop that I would be leaving the parish and the ministry. In view of an earlier conversation I had had with him he wanted to open up again the whole business of my finding it impossible to believe the basic doctrines of Christianity. He seemed to be convinced that my problem had to do with Jennifer's death and that it would pass. He kept quoting Jesus on the cross: 'My God, my God why hast thou forsaken me?' 'If Jesus temporarily lost his faith why shouldn't you? Give it time.'

I knew there was no point, I had been agonising over these things for years and when I finally came to the decision to leave I felt a wonderful sense of relief, a feeling of freedom; I no longer felt myself compromised, I was no longer a hypocrite. Furthermore, since not long after Jennifer had died I'd been having a relationship with Kate, who had been a friend to both of us. Her sensible and gentle understanding and her unwillingness to be judgmental of Jennifer in the utter torment of her last alcohol-sodden months were remarkable. She had been such a support to me during the trauma of Jennifer's last years and afterwards. While Jennifer was alive Kate and I were simply friends whose concern was for Jennifer's wellbeing. However, not long after her death we both realised that for both of us there was much more to it than that.

Since the announcement that I would be leaving the parish and the ministry had been made, I received every kind of reaction of which it was possible to conceive. Some of these were communicated to me non-verbally and some parishioners told me straight out. One man shook my hand firmly and said:

'I'm sorry you're going and whatever you do good luck.' Mrs Bowers the parish busybody, who had given me torment over the years, without uttering a word communicated to me that she would be delighted to see the back of me! I found it within myself to feel sorry for her and hoped that I did not communicate to her that the truth was that I would not miss her either. I did hope that she would give my successor an easier time than she had given me, but I had my doubts.

I knew that for some, who wouldn't have had the confidence to articulate it, I had their good wishes and I had no doubt others thought that compared with their departing rector Judas was only in the ha'penny place.

I had no idea how my clerical colleagues felt about why I was leaving the ministry. In the early days of my doubt it became obvious to me that any of them I knew well enough to broach the topic with didn't want to know. Even particular friends made it obvious that they were uncomfortable with my questions and doubts and would quickly change the subject. However, one colleague whom I didn't know well, once mentioned the topic himself and in an offhand kind of way said: 'Maybe you're right.' I soon came to the point that I would never initiate discussion of belief, and if somebody else did I would let them make the running unless they asked me a direct question when I would answer it honestly but briefly.

It didn't matter to me what other people thought. I knew where I stood, acknowledged to myself that my new position too was a belief, but that it was a perfectly legitimate way to try to make sense of the mystery that is life on this planet in this unfathomable universe. In a religion-obsessed society to be an atheist was to be a pariah. It did make me uncomfortable with people I liked and respected who did not understand, but finally I comforted myself that if it was a problem for them it was not my responsibility to try to solve it.

One morning shortly after the news was out that I was leaving, I was sitting in my study when a car drove up to the front door. It was Father Keane the elderly parish priest. We had always worked well together and we had co-operated in doing many things. He had been particularly fond of Jennifer and she of him. I opened the hall door before he had time to ring the bell. He said not a word. He put out his hand and shook mine firmly. His eyes filled and a tear ran down his cheek. Still holding his hand I brought him into the hall and led the way to the kitchen where I put on the kettle. When I was able to I thanked him for coming. He said gently and slowly:

'I know it may sound incongruous to you, but I want wish you God's blessing wherever you go and whatever you do. You did a wonderful job in this parish.' Through welling tears I said simply:

'Thank you. You will never know what that means to me.' I made a pot of tea and we talked. Our conversation was summed up when I said:

'I can do no other,' and he replied:

'I know. I understand.'

Since deciding to leave I often wondered where I might be now if I had not left the bank, where I had worked after I left school, to train for ordination. I did not suffer under the illusion that I would have been a financial high flyer, a high executive or a pundit at head office. I might, however, have been a manager in a small country branch or even a suburban one. I would not have been married to Jennifer, whom I met at university. I might well have married Maura Murray, who had also worked at the bank. I went out with her for the best part of a year and I was very fond of her. A son of Maura's had turned up at the rectory a short time before Jennifer died claiming that I was his father. He was probably right; it was perfectly possible. Having refused to give him money he hadn't been in touch for some time. It is interesting and often amusing to speculate on the might-have-beens in life but it is never wise to allow them to carry too much weight.

Jennifer's death had come unexpectedly and brought to an abrupt end the hope I had been nursing for years that she might recover from her addiction to alcohol that had destroyed our marriage and her life. It destroyed one of the most admirable people I had ever known. Jennifer was intelligent, honest and as one of her drinking companions had said to me at her funeral: 'She was a lady, she treated everyone equal.'

After the maelstrom of Jennifer's life of alcohol, and the ambivalence I felt between the fact that she was now free of the demon that had destroyed her and the gap that her death had left in my life, I began slowly to put together something of a new way of living. During the months since her death Kate had become a wonderful support and an important part of my life, and I of hers. She had been deserted some years before by her husband who had run away with a parishioner of mine and left her to rear their young daughter, Siobhán, on her own.

I was leaving the parish with no job to go to but with somewhere to live. Mary and Tom, my daughter and her husband, had found a flat at a reasonable rent in Dublin. When I was installed there I would be in a better position to look for a job. I was prepared to do anything within reason. I would be a car journey of an hour or so from Kate. She would keep her job as a school teacher for the moment and we would assess things when I had found work in Dublin. The dilemma was that Kate believed that the time to sell her house and move to Dublin was when Siobhán was a little older, but Kate and I did not want to wait much longer before we moved in together. In the meantime it would not be a good idea for me to return to the parish at weekends to stay with Kate and Siobhán. I wouldn't mind bumping into former parishioners, with a few exceptions, but some of them mightn't be too keen to bump into me. Furthermore it would not be fair, for one reason or another, to the new rector.

I had stayed overnight with Kate the night before the furniture van was to come. I was up early and at the rectory in good time before it was due to arrive. I had already sent for sale all the large pieces of furniture that Jennifer and I had bought at auction when we had moved into the rectory. Nobody then wanted big old furniture of the kind that was suitable for us to furnish the large rooms of the rectory. Most of the time I felt no emotion or sentimentality about things that had strong associations with Jennifer. However, every now and again, totally unexpectedly, something would throw me. The association of an item would whip me back to earlier happier days and sadness would wash over me and stop me in my tracks. In the meantime there had been too much unhappiness and pain to allow such memories to survive for long. I was much more vulnerable to memories of the children, but they had left home so long ago that there were few of these and they had never lived in this house.

When the van had gone I walked around the empty rooms to be sure that nothing had been left behind. I was soon overcome by a confusion of powerful emotions that I had no instinct to disentangle. They were primarily emotions of loss, great sadness and on an overweening sense of futility. I cried, for what exactly I wasn't sure; for Jennifer, for my own loss, for the pain and suffering of the world in the face of no credible account as to why it should be. I was, however, confirmed in my view that I could not accept the answers that religious people offered to these questions and reconciled myself to the fact that I would have to live with the mystery and in due course die with it too.

I pulled the hall door behind me. After I turned the car in front of the house I passed the entrance to the stable-yard where I had found Jennifer on that awful night. I drove slowly down the avenue for the last time to the total unconcern of the sheep grazing in the field on either side. I turned right onto the road and as I passed the churchyard I felt that I was leaving Jennifer behind. I drove to Kate to tell her I was on my way. She was the only hope I had to give purpose to my future.

CHAPTER 2

I arrived at the flat in a northside Dublin suburb before the furniture van and when they came I was ready to direct them to where they should put things. It became clear to me quickly that despite having sent the larger pieces of furniture to auction I had kept too much. I would have to come to terms with living in a smaller space than I had been used to. When the men had emptied everything from the van into the flat they departed and left me feeling disorientated. There was a musty smell and a feeling of damp. I opened the windows. Everything about my new accommodation was smaller. A child was crying in the flat above and on the street outside the window there was a bus stop where busses pulled up with squealing brakes and accelerated loudly as they drew away.

My first thought was to phone Kate to tell her I had landed. I thought however that I ought to let Mary know first that I had arrived, since it was she who had found the flat for me.

'Mary.'

'Hi Dad.'

'I've arrived, but I've brought too much furniture.'

'I thought you might.'

I had told Mary and Peter what a support Kate had been to me when things with their mother had been bad. I hadn't told them what had transpired between us since Jennifer died, but I would when it was opportune. There would be plenty of time.

'I'll come around this evening and give you a hand to sort things out.'

'I'm in no hurry, but that would be a great help.'

The trauma of the uprooting suddenly assailed me. The problem of the furniture became the piece of practicality that I could talk about. I phoned Kate from the chaos of an alien place.

'I brought too much furniture.'

'I'd hold on to it if you can. You may move to somewhere bigger when you find your feet. I can't wait for the weekend; I miss you already.'

'I miss you too.'

There hadn't been time for fresh local news since I had seen Kate, but we talked on for a while, mostly about Siobhán.

'She told me this afternoon that now that you had gone I wasn't to rely on her for company; she had her own friends.'

I felt sorry for Kate. She had been heroic since Conor left; her whole life had been for Siobhán. Kate knew she couldn't make up for the fact that her father had deserted her, but she did everything she could to compensate. Now this, at a time when Kate deserved a bit of ease. We talked for quite a while about Siobhán, my migration to the city, my new accommodation and the hundred and one small things that lovers talk about, no matter what their age. When we hung up I made the bed and felt like getting into it, but it was only late afternoon and Mary was coming over later, so I went out to explore the area.

It was the north side of the city which was unfamiliar to me; when I was in college I lived on the south side of the river. My landlady of those days admitted occasionally to venturing across the river to shop, but averred that she never felt safe until she was back on the south side. My new environment was a middle class residential area of semi-detacheds. The house I had come to had been converted into two flats. There was a well kept park a few streets away where the smell of cut grass brought me back to the old croquet lawn at the back of the rectory. I sat on a bench watching a group of boys doing tricks on their bicycles. I hadn't done anything yet about finding a job so until I found one I would sign-on to the dole. Mary had told me where the nearest Social Welfare Office was. I planned to go there first thing in the morning. I rambled back towards the flat and on the way picked up some groceries at a supermarket. I made scrambled egg and read for a while. Mary arrived and I was glad to see her, but I was too tired to start finding places for things. We talked for a while and when she left I went straight to bed. I kept falling asleep and the noise of buses at the stop outside kept waking me. Eventually I slept and woke early in the morning having slept as well as I had done for a long time.

I phoned Kate before she went to work and without saying anything in particular to do so she reassured me simply with the sound of her voice and the warmth of her tone. After a mug of coffee for breakfast I went to look for the Social Welfare Office. I was there early and there were only two people before me in the queue. When I arrived at the hatch and gave my social insurance number the clerk asked me a lot of questions. It was clear that he didn't have many clergymen arriving to sign-on! The first thing he wanted to establish was whether I had been made redundant. When he was sure that this was not the case he wanted to know if I had been fired or had I left voluntarily. It was clear to me that the young man had not been long in the job. The next question he asked was whether I would be looking for work as a clergyman. Having established that I was prepared to work at anything within reason he seemed to have been struck dumb. There was a long silence which I broke by pointing out to him that I was not strong enough to be a labourer, and I was going to say but didn't: and not smart enough to be a neuro-surgeon but anything in between would do. I felt it was too early in the day for humour. He suddenly stood up and said: 'Stay there,' and went through a door at the back of the office. After what seemed an age the clerk returned. He sat down and said:

'The trouble is that your contributions don't entitle you to unemployment benefit.'

'But I've been contributing for years.'

'Yes but you are in a category that covers everything else except unemployment.' It suddenly hit me: nobody ever thought that a clergyman would be unemployed. I thanked the young man and, no doubt to the relief of the queue that had built up behind me, I left the office.

I went back to the flat and phoned Church Administration. I asked to speak to somebody who would know about these things. An understanding woman came on the line and I explained my position. She asked me to hold on and when she came back she said:

'That's correct. When social insurance for clergy was started, unemployment wasn't included. Given the shortage of clergy I suppose it wasn't envisaged that there would ever be unemployed clergy.'

'What if a clergyman had sexually assaulted someone or had embezzled the parish funds?'

'I suppose the Church thought that her clergy would never be involved in such things, or if they were it could be covered up and a discreet move to another parish would solve the problem. The most likely possibility was that the presumption of clergy respectability was so great that nobody thought about it at all.'

'That's no good to me.' I muttered under my breath. I thanked her, put down the phone, sat staring into space and then went and made myself another mug of coffee. The gun was to my head. I would have to find some kind of work quickly.

The following day I returned to the Social Welfare Office and was glad to speak to an older woman. She was kindly and simply asked me what my skills were.

'I'm literate, numerate and I can walk and talk,' I said flippantly. She smiled:

'Have you any training or qualifications?'

'I have a degree in Latin, philosophy and theology.' She looked up at me from the form she was completing, smiled and said:

'Are you sure you're in the right place?'

'To be honest' I said,' I have a habit of finding myself in the wrong place, so I'm probably not.'

'Could you teach?' she asked, going, I felt, beyond her terms of reference, but trying to be helpful.

'I haven't a teaching diploma and there aren't many schools that want Latin, philosophy or theology. I was thinking more of a job as a clerk, a store man or,' feeling flippant again, probably from embarrassment, when I had no good reason to be since I needed badly to earn some money, 'I could be a lollipop man.' She smiled and before she had time to say anything, in order to affirm that I really was deadly serious about trying to find any kind of job, I said:

'I could drive a van.'

'Have you a commercial driving licence?' the woman asked.

'No, and to be honest I'm not a great driver.'

'Give me your telephone number and leave it with me, and I'll phone you if I come up with anything.'

I left the Welfare Office for the second time; the first time I was deflated, this time I was verging on panic. The reality was that I had no income and by the look of things it might be some time before I secured one. I was living off the hump of a cheque that the parish had given me when I left. At the rate I was spending money on rent and food I would be penniless in four or five weeks and I had a bank loan to repay. After I had sold my twelve-year-old car, as I intended to do, I could survive for another few weeks after that.

I had rejected the idea that I might ask Derek, the husband of Jennifer's old college friend Heather, now a successful businessman, about a job but things were looking so bleak that I changed my mind. Derek was a pleasant enough fellow and I always found him reasonably congenial company, but we had little in common. We had different perspectives on life, expressed in shorthand: he business, and I people. On the rare occasions when we met we never discussed these things, but I had no doubt that that was what it came down to, and if I am honest with myself, I didn't admire some of his attitudes, but he did give a great deal of employment.

I swallowed my pride and phoned. His secretary told me he was away on business and wouldn't be back for a week. As all good secretaries do she asked if she could take a message. I declined, thanked her and hung up. I was glad in a way that I hadn't been able to speak to him and thought that by the time he arrived back I might have found something and not be beholden.

I had no idea how to begin to look for a job. I could walk in off the street to businesses and hope that, despite having no useful qualifications, a moderately civilised presentation of myself might impress some employer.

I kept an eye on ads in the newspaper and saw one for an assistant in a plumbers' supplier. A few days after I had answered it I had a phone call from a woman to make an appointment for an interview. I had answered the ad in such a way that I didn't declare that I didn't know much more about the business than the difference between a tap and a lavatory cistern. I knew, however that I could learn.

I was shown into the office of the manager. He was considerate and knew immediately that he wasn't dealing with the average store assistant. In summary I was up front with him – degree in useless subjects, no experience in plumbing matters, willing to learn and above all needing to earn a wage. As I had squared with him he did the same with me:

'I'm sorry to put you to the trouble of coming for an interview, but I'm looking for somebody with experience in the business or somebody young that can be trained.' He was kind and we talked about many things. He was in no hurry for me to go. Eventually he said:

'If I come across anything that might suit you I will get in touch.' He checked my contact details, walked to the outer door with me and wished me well.

I went for an interview for the job as a school janitor and in contrast to the plumbers' supplier manager, the vice-principal, a man much younger than me, was patronising and condescending and ended by saying:

'I'm sorry you are simply not suitable for this job. Thank you for coming.'

I was hopeful that I might have some chance when I went for an interview for a job managing a research project that involved co-ordinating the work of three departments at one of the institutes of technology. Having a degree, thought I, would be a help. No such luck. A month after the interview I received a 'the post has been filled' duplicated letter personalised with my name and address.

Having been to numerous interviews I began to feel that my best hope was to contact Derek. Even if he could give me some job until I found something more permanent.

I phoned him at home. Heather answered the phone. Before I had time to explain what I was on about she invited me around for lunch on Sunday. Kate was coming up at the weekend, and although I had told her about Derek and Heather she hadn't met them and this was a good opportunity for them to know about her.

'A friend of Jennifer, Kate, is coming for the weekend. Will it be all right if we both come?'

'Of course, she'd be welcome.'

When Kate phoned that evening, as she did every evening because the coinbox of the phone in the hall was jammed, her natural pragmatism consoled me somewhat, that, given time, I would inevitably find something suitable. I told her about Sunday lunch with Derek and Heather. Despite everything I told her about them she said:

'I look forward to meeting them.' Kate would make up her own mind. She arrived on Saturday morning, not willing to leave Siobhán more than one night in the house with two friends who were staying, both in their early teens. Kate left her with the assurance of safety in numbers and a promise not to have anyone else into the house.

Despite knowing the area and my descriptions of the flat, Kate was taken aback at how small it was. I had anticipated her and said:

'It'll do until I sort myself out.'

Sunday lunch was the best meal I'd had since I had come to the city. Kate and Heather hit it off, chiefly on the grounds of each having known Jennifer at different stages of her life. Both of them steered away from Jennifer's drinking and talked about her best qualities while I was listening to Derek who was his usual expansive and self-satisfied self. Anytime we met he was effusive about what a bijou house the rectory was.

'The parish will probably sell it.' I said, 'it isn't suitable as a modern rectory.'

'Why not?'

'Like any old house it's expensive to maintain and there's always something that needs to be done. Furthermore there aren't many clergy wives that will live in a house that needs large furniture and is hard to heat and to keep.'

'If it were nearer to the city I'd buy it myself. What lovely grounds and that stable-yard, not that I'd keep horses mind you.'

I didn't want to put a damper on the social aspect of our lunch but I had phoned in the first place hoping to ask Derek about a job. It went against the grain, but I was becoming desperate and in a gap in the conversation I broached the subject:

'Derek, I haven't been able to find a job and I wonder if you would have one available. I'm prepared to do anything.' He didn't respond, so that I wondered if he had heard me. I waited.

'Will the Church not help to find you something? Any kind of job I might have would not be suitable for a man in your position.'

'The only position I'm in is that I'm almost broke. I left the ministry because I found I couldn't believe the stuff any longer, so I'm responsible for myself. The Church owes me nothing. I'm unemployed and I need work in order to live.'

'Should you not have found something to do before you resigned?'

'The shyster,' I thought to myself. 'That's no help to me now.'

'That's why you're where you are and I'm where I am,' I said, 'I'm not cute enough,' and I felt like adding 'and you know what you can do with your job?' I was, however, cute enough to keep that bit to myself.

'If you come in to the office in the morning, say ten o'clock, I'll see what I can do.'

'The bollocks,' I thought. 'He's going to interview me like some youngster that answered an advertisement in the paper, or he's going to pass me on to somebody else to do the same,' but since paupers can't be picky, I had no option but to agree.

I turned up at Derek's office at the appointed time on Monday morning. His secretary told me he was on the phone and to take a seat. I sat down and the secretary brought me a morning paper. After a while Derek emerged from his office:

'Ah John, sorry to keep you waiting.'

'Sorry to bother you,' I said, hoping he would say: 'It's no bother at all,' but he didn't. To give him his due I don't think he really saw me as a nuisance.

'Come in.' He stood back to let me into his office. It was square with a huge desk at one side with a large leather-covered swivel chair. There were two easy chairs, to one of which Derek ushered me. He sat in the other.

'John, are you sure there isn't something you can do more suited to you than what I can offer?'

'I'm sure there is, but I cannot afford to wait to find it. I've been to interviews with no luck. I need to have a job to pay the rent.'

'Well there is something I can offer you that will keep you going until you find something suitable. We need a reliable checker in the warehouse. It involves checking goods as they are taken out of containers. It won't stretch you; it's straightforward. Will you have a look at it?'

'Certainly I will.' Derek went to his desk, pressed a button and asked his secretary to send up Mick Quinn.

'This man is the warehouse foreman. He'll bring you down and show you what's involved.' The foreman arrived. 'Mick I have someone here that's interested in the checker job, will you bring him down and show him around,' and to me he said: 'Come back to me when you're ready.'

Mick brought me downstairs. On the way he asked me if I had done anything like this kind of work before. When I told him I hadn't he asked me what kind of work I had done. I was stumped for a second and then stuttered something about working with people rather than things. I don't know what he made of it but he didn't pursue it any further. He was bound to have known from my having been with the boss who asked me to go back to him that I wasn't your average blue-collar job applicant.

He brought me to a large yard with a vast warehouse at the end. There were two massive container trucks reversed up to the door which was almost the width of the building. Men were unloading pallets from the containers while a man in a brown coat was ticking off items on a clipboard. Mick waited until there was a gap in these proceedings when he brought me up onto the ramp:

'Eddie this is, I didn't get your name?'

'John.'

'This is John, he's interested in the checker job. Will you show him what it's about?' Eddie went through the procedure of checking items out of the container with me and then brought me to a small office at the entrance and showed me how to compare the results with a bill of lading.

The only question I had was to know how one could be sure to identify correctly the goods on the pallet, to know the name and identify them on the bill of lading.

'It's obvious most of the time, and if you're in any doubt you can ask one of us.'

I thanked the checker and Mick, who was concerned that I would find my way and went back to Derek's office. His secretary phoned through to say I was there. Derek came to the door and ushered me in.

'Well, what do you think?'

'I'd be happy with that; it's straightforward and won't stretch me.'

'Good. You can take it until you find something more suitable.'

I started on the following Monday and worked for the morning with Eddie the checker who had shown me how. In the afternoon I was on my own and found it straightforward enough. Having to be in to work on time and leaving at 5.00pm every day I found strange. I had not worked to the clock since I was in the bank before I went to college, but now at least I could pay the rent and buy food. Kate had offered to help if I were stuck, but I was greatly relieved that I would not have to call on her. For the first time in my life I was a member of a trade union and was proud of it.

I still had difficulty identifying some of the goods on the pallets and was assured by Eddie that from time to time items were left off the bill of lading, but to be sure to ask him; he would know if they were all right.

After about six weeks when I was well into the job, one morning at about ten past eight three Garda cars swung into the yard. They drove up to the entrance to the warehouse; Guards jumped out and ordered us all to stand back against the wall while others began to search the warehouse systematically and the container that we were unloading. It suddenly hit me; the items that weren't on the bill of lading! We were all, one at a time brought over to the office and interrogated by two Guards in plain clothes.

By lunchtime Mick, Eddie and two others had been arrested and taken away. A youngster, one of the fork-lift operators and I were told we could go. The warehouse was closed and Guards stood at the entrance. On the way home later in the afternoon, I went into a café to have a cup of coffee to collect myself. A man came in and sat down at a table across from me and opened an evening paper. The banner headline read: **'DRUG SEIZURE; CLERGYMAN QUESTIONED'**.

Jennifer had always told me that I was too trusting of what I read in the papers, that journalists were more interested in a good story than in the truth of it or the effect it had on people. She used to say that tabloid journalists were a low form of life. The headline, however, was entirely accurate, but it wasn't by any means the whole story, or even the most important part of the story, but it was the bit that would sell newspapers.

I left the café and bought a paper. The article did say that four people had been arrested, but I had been released after questioning. The rest of the article was accurate. My first thought was to contact Mary and my son Peter. I went to a phone box and phoned them both in work and explained what had happened. Peter asked how they knew that I was a clergyman. Had I told them? I hadn't told anybody. As far as I was aware nobody in work knew, but it's not the kind of thing one could hide for long. I had no idea how it had come out. That was irrelevant now; the press found out some way and had exploited it for their purposes.

By the time I had phoned Kate she was just in from school. I told her the facts of the matter in the certain knowledge that a distorted version, that would lose nothing in the telling, would circulate in the parish before nightfall. There is no purchase for people if the story they tell is not sensational. A mundane and ordinary story does not bring kudos to the teller any more than it sells newspapers. We both thought immediately of Mrs Bowers who, when the topic was mentioned, would say something like: 'I knew he was up to something. He had no interest in the flowers for the church.' I also thought of Kathleen, a parishioner, the neurotic recluse whose husband Bill I could imagine pronouncing on the matter in a few well chosen words to anyone who was prepared to listen:

'Bloody lies. That man would be no more involved in that kind of thing than he'd fly. I don't give a curse what the papers say.'

I had no option but to sit it out; the whole thing would be a nine days' wonder. Those who knew me would know that the innuendo had no substance and others were free to make of it what they would.

A number of people made contact with me to be supportive. Amongst them, to give him his due, was the bishop, a few of my former clerical colleagues, a couple of people from the parish and some friends. Derek was badly shaken by the effect the whole thing would have on his business, and was understanding and apologetic for the adverse effect the publicity would have on me.

I went into work the following morning on the assumption that the warehouse would be open again. It wasn't. There was still a police guard, but I was told that it would be open after lunch. I turned up then to find that in a few months I had gone from being a defunct cleric from a small parish in the country to chief checker in a large import business in the city. My status as chief checker required of me that afternoon to train in to the job two young clerks from the office upstairs. At that stage it was clear that Mick and Eddie would not be back.

The newspapers the following morning were clear that I had known nothing about what had been going on at the warehouse. Kate and I decided that at the weekend I would go down and stay with her for the first time since I had left. I would not disport myself in public, but I would not hide either. It was a strange sensation driving into the parish. I remembered the first time that Jennifer and I had been to meet the nominators before I was appointed. We had been at one about how much we liked the house. I wouldn't want to go back to see it now even though a successor had not yet been appointed. Neither would I go to the churchyard. Jennifer had had no time for visiting graves. She would say:

'What's left of people is in your heart and your head and a patch of earth has nothing to do with it.' She had left strict instructions that I was not to erect a headstone.

I drove around the back of the house and Kate saw me from the kitchen. She was into the yard before I stood out of the car. She stopped and watched as I approached; her smile lifted my heart. We hugged tightly and held each other without a word. We separated enough to see each other's smiles that said that we were both mystified that we should be lucky enough at this stage of our lives to share such joy. We held hands like teenagers and went inside. In the kitchen we kissed. Kate pulled away.

'We'd better wait, Siobhán may be in.' She put on the kettle. She'd have made a wonderful clergyman's wife; at the first sign of somebody coming she made tea. We sat and talked sharing the little things of our lives since we were last together, going over again many of the things we had already talked about on the phone.

'After this week-end I'll tell Siobhán about us.'

'I have no doubt she already knows.'

'I'm sure she does, but I owe it to her to tell her.'

In the evening when Siobhán arrived home she came into the kitchen to say 'hello'. She was sullen and just about civil, and went straight to her room.

On the Saturday morning I walked down to the village for the paper. Owen, in the shop, greeted me:

'Begod your reverence it didn't take you long to find fame after lavin' us.'

'I don't have to tell you, Owen, it wasn't the kind of fame I'd look for.'

'Sure doesn't the whole countryside know that you wouldn't be up to that kind of thing? I suppose those fellas'll get a big sentence.'

'I can't comment. I've been told that I may have to give evidence in Court.' There was nobody else in the shop and I hoped I would not bump into anyone else I knew on the way back to Kate's and I didn't.

Our chief concern was Siobhán. Kate was weathering as best she could the turbulence of Siobhán's early teenage years. It wasn't easy. She was barely civil to me as she knew that I would be on her mother's side, but I said nothing; I did not interfere. I was able to support Kate when we were together as I remembered clearly when Mary went through a similar phase, and I had seen a number of times the mayhem caused in parishioner's homes by volatile teenagers, especially girls with their mothers.

'I know it's not easy, but it's a phase and they all come through it,' I tried to assure Kate.

'Yes but you and Jennifer had each other, and what's more she blames me that her father left. She doesn't remember him, and he has made no attempt to see her. She thinks that if he were here she'd have a better life; he'd understand her better than I do.'

After a wonderful weekend with Kate the time approached for me to leave. It brought me back to those Sunday evenings when I was at boarding school. At the end of a long week-end at home I would be overcome by a kind of nausea as the time approached for me to pack my bag to go back to school.

I was at my post as chief checker in the warehouse first thing on Monday morning.

CHAPTER 3

I was, *de facto*, chief checker as I was the only one left apart from the two new ones. The other two had been sacked and even if they had not been, they were not free to come to work; they were on remand in prison pending the hearing of their bail application. None of the buggy drivers or the youngster who kept the warehouse tidy were up to the checker job, so it had fallen to me to train in the two who had been sent down from the office. We were under strict instructions to call the Guards if we found anything that looked even remotely suspicious.

A couple of weeks after the new checkers had started, one of them came to me and asked me to look at a number of boxes that didn't seem right. I went and looked. He was right, they looked suspicious, so I didn't touch them and phoned the Guards. Two plain clothes officers arrived. I knew one of them immediately and he knew me:

'Hello, your Reverence. Is this where you are?'

He had been stationed in the county town near my former parish and had come to the village to investigate when someone had broken into the vestry of the church and damaged the safe. I couldn't remember his name. We talked for a while before he joined his colleague in the container with the suspicious boxes. They opened the boxes checked the list and found that in fact they were all okay.

'Better to be sure than sorry,' my friend's colleague said. 'Don't hesitate to call us again,' and the two drove away.

The following Monday morning a Garda car drove into the yard and the passenger stood out. It was my friend who had investigated the vestry break-in.

'Hello, your Reverence. Have you a minute?'

'Yes, of course.'

'My wife is district sergeant where you used to be. I was telling her I met you. There's something she thought it would be no harm for you to know. The young lady Siobhán could be heading for trouble. She's in with a bad crowd. My wife has spoken to her mother, but there's no change. There's going to be a bust soon and it would be better for her if she wasn't around. I suspect that she's being led. She's out of her depth.'

'Is it drugs?'

'Yes.'

'What do I do?'

'Get her mother to lock her in her bedroom if necessary, but keep her away from the crowd she's with. She's probably only using, but one of them is supplying and that's serious. My wife tells me that her mother doesn't seem to be able to control her. Sorry to bring this kind of news.' We talked on for a short time about young people, drugs and the world we live in. Mine were reared and long gone and he and his wife hadn't started.

'I hope you don't mind me telling you about this.'

'On the contrary, I'm grateful to you that you did. Leave it with me; I'll do what I can.'

I had to tell Kate exactly what the Guard had told me, and quickly; I had no way of knowing how soon the police swoop would be. On the way home from work in the bus I felt an emptiness. Just when my life was beginning to give me some form and routine, the life of the one person in the world who cared deeply for me and gave my life a new meaning, was in trouble. Just as Kate and I were feeling secure together her life was being undermined. Siobhán's attitude to me had always been ambivalent. I was hardly a good role model as a father. Her own father, who she didn't remember, had deserted her. I had to assume that she resented me and I didn't blame her. Kate had tried to talk to her about me as a prelude to declaring the real nature of our relationship, but Siobhán would have none of it; she would clam up and if Kate persisted she would walk away.

I went down to stay with Kate and Siobhán the week-end after the warning from the Guard. I had told Kate about it on the phone, but told her I didn't think she should say anything to Siobhán until we could discuss it. Siobhán was upstairs in her room when I arrived, so Kate and I could talk.

'Did you know she was taking drugs?'

'I did, but she says it's only cannabis and that's harmless and she gave me the usual spiel about how it should be legalised as it is in Holland. You know all the things that young people say despite what research has shown. I can't get through to her.'

'Somehow you'll have to stop her seeing the group she knocks around with.'

'The only way I can do that is tell her why, and she will tell them. As far as she's concerned they're her friends, they're all great people and adults don't understand.'

School summer holidays for Kate were starting within a few days so she planned that she and Siobhán would go to her home place in County Cork until they heard that the Guards had made their raid.

'If she ever has the slightest indication of why we're going she'll never forgive me for not telling her.'

Kate and Siobhán could not stay in Cork for ever and the Garda bust had not taken place by the time they had to return home. Without telling Siobhán why, Kate had warned her about her friends and they had an unholy row in the train coming home. It was then that Kate finally decided that they would move to Dublin as soon as possible. She had been thinking about it anyway and this made the decision for her.

Kate recounted to me what happened on the evening of the Monday after Kate and Siobhán arrived home from Cork. Their door bell rang. Kate answered it to be met on the doorstep by a male and a female Guard.

'We have a warrant to search your house,' the man said holding out to Kate an official looking piece of paper. Kate stood back and let the Guards in.

'Is there anybody else in the house?'

'Yes, my daughter is upstairs.'

'Will you ask her to come down please?' Kate called up the stairs and Siobhán arrived down to the hall to be confronted by the two Guards.

'Are you in possession of any banned substances?'

'You mean drugs,' Siobhán said defiantly. 'No I am not, and you can search my room if you want.'

The female Guard asked Siobhán and Kate to step into the kitchen where she body searched Siobhán. She found nothing. Then she went upstairs to join her colleague who was searching Siobhán's room. They searched the bathroom, the other two bedrooms, and with her permission, Kate's room. They did a search of the downstairs rooms and the garage. They found nothing.

'That's it,' Kate said to Siobhán when the Guards had left. 'I'm selling this house and we're moving to Dublin.'

'I know why you want to move to Dublin.'

'Yes you do but I was waiting for your sake until you were older, but not now. You've had a narrow escape and it's time we both made a new start.'

On the spot Kate found the number, picked up the phone and called the local estate agent. Siobhán raised Cain:

'You're forcing me into exile to take me away from my friends. I'm not going. You can go on your own to your failed priest lover.' For the next few weeks Kate ignored Siobhán's vitriol that she alternated with long silences. To Kate this was no worse than her anxiety about the company she kept. Siobhán was finally chastened when one of her friends was charged with supplying, and in time was sentenced to six months in prison and two others received suspended sentences for possession.

Kate understood the loss that Siobhán, at her age, would feel at leaving her friends and did her best to ease her disappointment at having to move. Deep down Siobhán knew that loyalty to her friends would lead to trouble but she regurgitated all the usual arguments for legalising cannabis. Society, parents and everyone in authority didn't understand. It was a simple matter of common sense: 'look at Holland.'

Kate's house sold quickly and well. I found two houses that might be suitable and Kate particularly liked one in a nearby estate. By the end of August Kate, Siobhán and I had moved in.

Between the rectory and my Dublin flat I had been living for more than a year on my own. Before that I had lived with Jennifer in the last years of her enslavement to alcohol and had deluded myself that she would finally defeat her addiction. This delusion diminished as time passed and I was holding on to it by only a thread when her accident, resulting from a drunken stupor, happened. It triggered her decline and led quickly to her death. For the last few years of her life we had lived together under the same roof but estranged. It was worse than that. There was no conversation of any kind other than about food, clothing and shelter; the essentials of the bare subsistence that enabled us to live each in our separate hell.

In the early months after Jennifer's death I had lived in a vacuum, without the responsibility I had felt to hold things together as best I could. It transpired that I had been living a hopeless delusion that things might have improved or even taken a dramatic turn for the better. This had become for me a *raison d'être* that had tragically gone. I was forced to ask myself what I was to do next and concluded finally that I should no longer be in the ministry. It also led me spontaneously to Kate and the warmth of her care which led to our love and intimacy that gave purpose again to my life.

Kate had slowly come to terms with the disappearance of Conor with the daughter of a former parishioner of mine. Kate had been Jennifer's friend, but despite her own travails she had been a wonderful support to me in mine.

Shortly after we had moved into the new house, one evening Siobhán assailed Kate with:

'How do you expect me to live in a rabbit warren like this?' I was amused at the irony of her using an analogy of the country to express her abhorrence of living in the city. I tried to point this out to her humorously, to lift her spirits a little, but she wasn't interested. She would not entertain anything that might diminish her protests and lost no opportunity to accuse Kate and me of ganging up against her.

'It's not easy for me either,' Kate said, 'I've never lived in the city before, but we'll get used to it. I've spoiled you to make up for your father not being around. You'll have to get used to adapting to things you wouldn't choose or you're going to make life hell for yourself and everyone around you.'

This was the first time in my company that Kate had spoken to Siobhán of Conor. She stomped out of the room and banged the door behind her. We had always conceded willingly that leaving her friends was difficult for her.

'It's not difficult. It's the end of my life,' she protested.

She went back to the country to stay with one friend a couple of times, but it wasn't the same. She came to know a girl in the Park where we lived who was already at the school that she would attend in September. The 'friends' issue, however, was finally resolved soon after school started; she found in her class a soul mate, Judy. In time tensions eased due mainly to Siobhán's friendship with Judy. A new, but only slightly less fraught, normality descended upon the house. We knew that the turbulence of Siobhán's adolescence would continue for some time, and we had no option but to weather it.

We, an unlikely three, were able to live more easily in the anonymity of a Dublin suburb than we would have been able to do in the small rural community we had left. In the country both Kate and I had resented the scrutiny, as teacher and rector, under which we had lived. Neither of us, however, had been prepared to trim our sails to the expectations of parents or parishioners. Of the trio in the house Kate was pivotal. She was the reason both Siobhán and I were there. Either of us could have been there without the other, but neither would have been there without Kate. Apart from anything else Kate owned the house and we were there by her grace and favour, not that she saw it that way. Siobhán and I were at worst forced to tolerate each other and at best to make living together reasonably pleasant. I certainly hoped to achieve the second. How Siobhán felt about it I could only speculate, but at this early stage I had a sense that her attitude was, at best, to put up with me.

Siobhán in the nature of things was moving from dependence on Kate to independence, a turbulent and painful process for both. Kate and I were affirming each other in the early stages of a mutual romantic life. It was the kind of thing more often associated with people of teenage years and early adulthood. The process of falling into this condition has traditionally been perceived as a device of evolution to attract people to each other in order to procreate the species. In our case the possibility of this was long since past. In the case of people of our age it is a hangover or over-run. Nature is not noted for her precision. In most of her manifestations she deals in exceptions and in some instances she is notably hit-and-miss. For the greater part of humanity the mysterious state of falling in love is the prelude to the mutual enjoyment of its natural consequence which leads to procreation and the onerous responsibility of rearing children. Without falling in love people would not have the same incentive to follow this inevitable consequence; procreation would be a matter of 'take it or leave it.' People might not bother to procreate, and the species would be in grave danger of dying out. Kate and I had all the mutual affirmation of being in love without the responsibility of raising children. Earlier in our lives we had both independently made our contribution to the next generation.

While feeling greatly for Kate as she coped with Siobhán's intermittent tempestuous outbursts, I had sympathy with Siobhán in her predicament, for predicament it was. She was caught between the imperative of adolescence, her mother's anxiety for her, which she considered unwarranted, and Kate's divided loyalty between her daughter and her lover. If I said anything that Siobhán interpreted as supporting her mother's point of view over against hers, something I tried not to do, it was inevitable that she would say to me: 'You're not my father,' to which neither Kate nor I would respond. It was of course true, but it carried a particular weight of significance that all of us understood. I felt I was disqualified from even mentioning Conor, and the topic arose between Kate and Siobhán only rarely and then usually in the heat of recrimination. The fact of the matter was that Conor had made no effort to see Siobhán since he left. Only recently, probably because of my presence in her life, had Siobhán raised with Kate the issue of meeting her father. Her interest was never sustained and became submerged under all the other emotional matters with which she was dealing.

Kate failed to find a permanent teaching job in Dublin, but she worked virtually full-time at supply teaching and hoped to secure a permanent post for the following school year. Supply teaching suited her well as it left her gaps between jobs which she was glad to use to order the house in such a way as it was comfortable and congenial especially for Siobhán, but also for herself and for me. On the material and financial level we managed well and Kate and I were on the same wavelength and entirely at ease with each other. My presence did not diminish one whit Kate's commitment to everything that it was possible to do as a mother to compensate as best she could to Siobhán for the absence of her father. Kate could accept why Conor left her; people do fall out of love and in love with someone else, just another of nature's idiosyncrasies. The hardest thing for Kate was to try to account in her own mind for why he might have abandoned so easily his only child.

Kate had had contact with Conor only through their solicitors to do with legal separation, signing over to her his share of the house and agreeing his contribution for maintenance for Siobhán. In all these matters he had been generous which did not surprise Kate. She was left, however, with the question as to why he had no interest in being in touch with his daughter whom he adored as a little girl. His solicitor didn't ask for access rights, but Kate was happy to give them and the Court granted them. Conor never sought to exercise them.

Kate could only speculate that Betty wanted him to cut off completely from Siobhán and from her. This was not consistent with the Betty that I knew as a parishioner who had given up running her family's farm to go away with Conor. Clergy, however, know only as much of parishioners as the parishioner wants them to know. In crisis or emergency many the rector has been astounded at what he has learned, and could never have suspected, about a parishioner he has known for years. Kate had no idea where Conor and Betty were. We had both heard rumours; the most credible one being Canada, but Kate had no reliable information. Betty was late in child-bearing age, but probably not beyond it. Should it ever transpire to be the case, Kate did not relish the prospect of telling Siobhán that she had half siblings.

My job at the warehouse was just that, a job. Though routine and often tedious it prevented me from becoming emasculated by complete financial reliance on Kate. It became clear that the job was mine for as long as I wanted it and I was grateful for that. Derek almost never appeared in the warehouse, and when he did we had only a passing conversation. He did however take to asking me up to his office occasionally. These visits were to make sure I was happy with the job and to reiterate to me in one way or another that it wouldn't lead anywhere. I became convinced by his attitude that he was genuinely concerned that 'a man in your position', as he used to put it, should be doing something more appropriate to my status than supervising the unloading of trucks. Even when I was in the ministry I didn't consider that I had a status. Other people did, especially some parishioners, but for much of the time I saw myself as doing a useful job. I saw myself as helping to create a healthy community; one that made a contribution to the larger community. I saw myself as being free to be with people in their joys and in their sorrows and to be supportive of people through the vicissitudes of life. Unfortunately the post that I then held required me to believe all kinds of metaphysical, magical doctrines of an earlier credulous age to which I finally found I could no longer subscribe. In the end when I accepted that I no longer believed these doctrines it came to me as an immense relief and gave me a peace and contentment like I hadn't had for many years.

CHAPTER 4

Fortunately for all of us Siobhán quickly settled in well to her new school. To say 'happily' would be too much. Siobhán wasn't ready to be happy about anything. Twice in her first week after she had finished her homework she went over to Judy's house which was in easy walking distance. They spent some time together on the first Saturday evening and Siobhán was home before ten o'clock. Kate wondered if they had fallen out already but she didn't comment and Siobhán didn't either.

One evening Kate lost patience with Siobhán:

'Your moods are making life hell for John and me.'

'Well just ignore them.'

'How can we ignore them? They poison the atmosphere.'

'Hell and poison are a bit much aren't they?'

'Believe me they are not. That's what it's like for us when you're in a mood.'

Siobhán did not reply, but things improved a little after that. She was more amenable to her mother and from time to time she was almost friendly to me. A routine became established to enable us each to pursue our own work. Kate taught, I checked containers and Siobhán went to school. On Saturday mornings Siobhán played basketball and Kate and I had a lie-in. On Sundays none of us went to church, chapel or meeting house. Kate and I went for a walk on the beach and prepared Sunday lunch together. Siobhán had not made her first holy communion so she hadn't been confirmed. Before she left the country Kate had stopped going to mass altogether and I was outside everything.

One evening Siobhán asked me:

'Why did you stop being a clergyman?'

She had never spoken to Kate or asked her anything about my leaving the parish, but perhaps she had picked up something locally. She hadn't seemed to us to be interested until now.

'Because I found I could no longer believe the teachings of the Church.'

'What teachings?'

'Most of them.'

'Like what?'

'That Jesus was God and that he rose from the dead.'

'What else?'

'That there's life after death. You can't be a clergyman unless you believe these things.'

'Huh,' and that was all. Siobhán asked no more questions. I felt it would not be opportune for me to say more unless she asked. When I recounted this conversation to Kate she was surprised.

'I often wondered that she had never commented. She probably thought you left because of us.'

Judy came often to the house. She was tall, lissom and kept her fair hair in a pony tail. She wore chunky sweaters, jeans and flat shoes. She exuded a quiet confidence beyond her years in who she was. She and Siobhán spent hours in Siobhán's bedroom doing whatever teenage girls do. There was always music. Kate frequently had to go upstairs to ask them to turn it down. Siobhán went over to Judy every Wednesday evening. Kate never asked any questions for the usual reason that parents don't ask questions: the more they ask the less they are likely to be told and in the hope that the converse will be true.

One Saturday night Siobhán announced:

'I'm going to a meeting with Judy in the morning.'

'What kind of a meeting?' Kate asked.

'What kind of a meeting do you think people go to on a Sunday morning?'

'Some kind of religious meeting, I suppose.'

'That's right.'

'Where is it?'

'In town. Judy goes there.' Kate, though curious, asked no more questions.

In the morning Siobhán was up early and left before half past nine. Kate and I went for our usual Sunday morning walk along the beach where I used to go when Jennifer and I spent summer holidays in Mary's house in Dublin. It was November. Siobhán's new departure was the topic that morning. Rain-laden clouds were threatening as we walked against the wind. We walked as briskly as the strong wind allowed and conversation was difficult. Back in the car we both felt the virtue of having struggled with the elements; the virtue of fresh air and exercise that conventional wisdom prescribes for a long and healthy life. We were just in time to avoid a sudden downpour that made the windscreen opaque. We sat and waited.

'Whatever it is, it's bound to be better than drugs,' Kate said.

'Anything is better than drugs.' The rain eased. I started the car, we picked up the papers and when we arrived home Siobhán was already there.

'How was your meeting?' Kate enquired.

'Fine. I don't know why you buy those Sunday papers.'

'They're quality papers I'll have you know,' I said lightly. 'No gutter press in this house. It's important to know what's going on in the world.'

'Is it?' Siobhán said.

Our Sunday morning pattern became established: Siobhán went with Judy to their meeting and Kate and I went for our walk and bought the papers on the way home. I knew exactly where her Sunday meeting had brought Siobhán. She had been emotionally manipulated by some preacher-man at a vulnerable stage in her life. It was, however, as Kate had said; better than drugs. This kind of religion reduced what for me was the mystery of our human existence to a simple but emotion-laden response to the challenge: will you give your life to the Lord? Implicit in this is the threat that if you don't you'll end up in hell. To accept this challenge is to accept the most incredible things with blind faith that are simply unbelievable from the perspective of reason. Millions of people in the world live with similar faith in the religion of their birth, Christian, Muslim, Hindu and many others. On the other hand, many people want what they believe about the mystery of the universe and our human existence to conform to at least a modicum of reason.

I did not want to undermine in any way what had brought Siobhán around to being easier to live with for her mother and me. In the emotional turmoil of her adolescence this kind of religious experience had given her some stability and purpose, no matter how incredible to me were the assumptions on which it was based. The longer I lived the more convinced I was that most of the metaphysical assumptions of religion were false but that the moral and social dimension of religion was of significant value in the world. If anybody wanted to bring up the topic with me I was quite happy to discuss it, but I was aware that religious belief, no matter how incredible to me, was important to many people. I did not want to undermine, let alone ridicule, that which gave meaning and purpose to the lives of so many.

It was clear that Kate and I were religiously in a different camp from Siobhán and Judy. Judy, when she was in the house, never broached these matters with us, but Siobhán brought it up from time to time. She occasionally directed questions to Kate, but seldom to me. I was glad to stay out of it.

'Do you not believe what it says in the Bible?' Siobhán asked. Kate sometimes had to teach RE in school, but by her own admission was not well informed about the Bible.

'I believe some of what it says but much of it is not the kind of thing it is possible to believe in this day and age.'

'The Bible is the Word of God.'

'I don't think it is quite as simple as that.'

'Our pastor is able to explain it better than I can.' Kate did not like being at variance with Siobhán who was coming around slowly to her mother after a long time of estrangement.

'Maybe I'll come with you one Sunday and listen to what your pastor has to say.'

When I heard this I had a fantasy that Kate would go one Sunday morning with Siobhán and Judy and come home for Sunday lunch having given her life to the Lord. It was an instantaneous fantasy. Kate was much too mature and balanced a person who knew her own mind to allow herself to be emotionally manipulated in this way.

Later that evening I said to her humorously: 'You want to mind yourself if you go to that religious meeting. They might convert you.'

'Don't worry, I can handle that,' she replied.

Over the years I had often wondered about religious experience and what it was about. How different kinds of personality made one person a rabid fundamentalist and another kind a High Church ritualist or one of the many religious types between. There were, too, many people who were entirely apathetic to religion and weren't in the slightest interested in it and people who were positively against religion.

'Why is it,' I asked Kate, 'that most people who belong to a religion affirm the religion into which they were born; the religion of their parents? Why is it that only an infinitesimal number of people convert by conviction from the religion of their birth to a different one? What does this tell us about what and how people believe?'

'What do you think?' Kate saw me as the religious expert.

'I think it tells us that indoctrination in early childhood is pretty indelible. Churches know what they are doing when they teach little children their own particular brand of religion, which of course is the only true one!'

'That's it,' she said, 'all the other religions have it wrong. At least these days they aren't killing each other or going to war as they did in the past, to make others conform.'

'Aren't they? What about Northern Ireland? What about the Nigerian civil war and the Iran/Iraq war? It's tribalism; a complex mix of religion and politics. No matter how sophisticated we think we are, there's a bit of it in all of us.'

'Religions indoctrinate,' I said. '"Teach", I suppose they would prefer to call it, to secure the loyalty of the next generation. As a trained teacher you know enough child psychology to know that the personality of the adult is largely determined by what they absorb in the early years when the child's mind is like a sponge. Most people accept religious propositions uncritically, without applying to them the kind of reason they apply in other areas of their lives. So obsessed with religion is the society that we were brought up in that if people do apply reason to their religious upbringing and find it incredible, they more often than not keep quiet about it not to upset other people or for some they don't talk about it because they're simply not interested.'

Strangely enough, Kate and I had never before discussed religion like this. She wanted to now so I continued along the lines:

'Whereas the social and ethical aspects of religion are important for people, the metaphysical and miraculous aspects are incredible for many more people than we imagine. Belief in the miraculous does, however, help some people to come to terms in some way with that universal human experience – the fear of death.'

Kate was brought up a Catholic and the Catholic Church is better at indoctrination than other Churches. In the past it laced its teaching with a large dose of guilt and fear. I noticed from time to time in Kate, despite her reason and common sense, a residual amount of both guilt and fear. Despite having rejected most of her early religious indoctrination, she would ask the 'what if' question.

'What if the Church has it right after all and there is a heaven and hell?' she posed. 'You might be better to hang in there just in case. There's nothing to lose and much to gain, but by rejecting everything one has little to gain in this life and the possibility, if it is all true, of a lot to lose in the next.'

'You take a punt on one or the other.' I said, 'that's what's called Pascal's wager. That's the kind of thing the preacher-man plays on. You want to be careful, if you go to his meeting he might resurrect your Catholic guilt and give you a Protestant way of getting rid of it.' Kate laughed.

'I'll chance it.'

Sometime later one Saturday Siobhán said to Kate:

'I told Judy I was explaining to you about the Bible and how it was the Word of God, and you said that one Sunday you might come to meeting with us.'

'And what did she say?'

'She thought it was a good idea: will you come in the morning?'

'Why not?'

Kate and I both liked Judy. She was a kindly and spoke to us with a gentle confidence. She had been brought up by her mother in the religion of this gospel hall. Her father never went and her mother, now in a wheelchair, went only occasionally. Judy was the youngest of her family; her brother and sister were married and gone.

Kate recounted to me the events of the Sunday morning in great detail. She and Siobhán left the house at Siobhán's usual time. They took the car, picked up Judy at the end of her road and drove into town. The meeting hall was in a small street in the centre of the city. They entered by a door in the wall, along a narrow passage, up a flight of fire escape-type steps to an entrance that led to a room laid out with seating for about fifty or sixty people. At the front there was a carpeted area a step or two up from the main part of the room. Here there was a lectern or prayer desk and a carved ecclesiastical-looking chair. Not having had to wait for a bus they were early. When they entered the room there were five or six elderly people standing at the back talking and at the lectern at the front there was a late-middle-aged man, tall, with grey hair and inclined to weight, standing at the lectern turning over the pages of a large Bible. He looked up and came down the room immediately.

Kate described him as an affable countryman with a Northern accent.

'Hello girls,' he said:

'Pastor, this is my mother.'

'You're very welcome. You're in the best of company; these are two fine young ladies.' Kate described how she had a wonderful feeling, a combination of pride and relief that Siobhán had come through such a difficult few years and now had a friend such as Judy, and to hear her described as a 'fine young lady.'

The three sat into a middle row, the pastor went back to the lectern and the room began to fill. There was the whole range of ages, but mainly older people, with a sprinkling of teenagers and some young couples with children. They all seemed to know each other and some of the older ones carried Bibles.

The service started. The pastor welcomed everybody and especially Kate as Siobhán's mother and gave the number of the hymn with a brief summary of its theme – joy in the Lord. The old lady on the harmonium started up and everyone sang lustily. At the end of the hymn the pastor read a passage from the Old Testament and expounded it. Then there was another hymn. The pastor read a passage from the New Testament, related it to the Old Testament passage in such a way as to show that the Bible was all of a piece; a direct communication from God, and that it held the answer to all the problems of life. The answer to the mystery and the problems of life was to give one's life to the Lord. Then he called on everybody to bow their heads and he led a long rambling prayer acknowledging people's need for Jesus and telling God that life without him was worth nothing and that people would end up in the halls of hell for all eternity if they didn't give themselves to Jesus. At the end of telling God a lot of things that you would expect him to know already there was another hymn. A child began to cry and could not be comforted. This continued in competition with the singing. Eventually, unable to comfort the child its father took the child out. The whole atmosphere of the service had been broken, so in a shorter form using the Bible, hymns, exhortations and prayers the pastor worked-up the congregation again to culminate in a climax. This climax was the exhortation to give one's life to Jesus who died to make people free, to steep one's life in the blood of the lamb that was sacrificed for the world so that everyone could have eternal life. For those who had already done this they were to do it again. He had worked the congregation to a spiritual orgasm that presumably the regulars indulged in every Sunday. For newcomers it was designed to encourage them to be born again and give their lives to Jesus as Lord and Master.

When Kate arrived home she was full of it and told me everything. She had been fascinated by the happy participation of the congregation in all that was going on, especially the singing of the hymns; their joyous faces and raised hands, Siobhán and Judy amongst them. She had not been moved to respond to the encouragement of the pastor to make a commitment to the Lord, but was glad to see Siobhán involved in this way of making sense of the mystery of the world rather than trying to escape from it, by taking drugs.

During the pastor's exhortations to the congregation, he had given an account of his own conversion many years before. Kate liked him. He was not a self-obsessed manipulator who was doing what he did because he could. He gave the impression that he had found the answer and wanted to share it with everybody. He had booked his place in heaven, as sure as one would book a seat in a theatre or on a train. He had no doubt where he was going when he died and he wanted everybody else to go there too.

Kate had never come across this kind of religion before. Her Catholic background had not brought her in contact with religion that wasn't part of the Church. She had of course heard of this kind of religious phenomenon but had never experienced it first hand.

'What do you make of it?' she asked.

'Conventicles like that are a reaction to the ponderous overpowering doctrine-obsessed institutional Churches.' I said, 'Churches for whom proof of their continuity with Jesus and the apostles is essential to prove the authenticity of their doctrines. For these evangelical groups the Bible is enough. They use the Bible, or rather those parts of it that suit their purpose, as a direct communication from God to prove what they believe; namely that to give meaning and purpose to life all you need to do is to give yourself to the Lord.'

'And is that not OK, if that's what people want?'

'Of course it is, but like every other version of religion, despite what adherents of them say, it is not amenable to reason. They teach and believe the most incredible things under the guise of faith. If their adherents question or are sceptical the answer is simple: they haven't enough faith.'

'What do you mean?'

'Most of the essential assumptions of religion come from a pre-scientific age and give answers based on faith in the miraculous and the magical. This kind of belief was common at a time when people did not have rational scientific answers to questions about the world. We don't need to believe these kinds of things nowadays because science gives us answers consistent with reason.'

Kate listened carefully and said:

'That's all very well, but you don't expect the average Joe Soap to get into all that kind of rational and scientific stuff. Give me some examples that the average person can understand.'

'Well it makes more sense to me to believe that the universe, for some mysterious reason, started as the scientists tell us with the Big Bang. It doesn't make any sense that it was created by a God who put human beings on one tiny planet in one small solar system in a universe of such immensity in which time and space merge and that our minds cannot fathom. Why would a God do that? It doesn't make sense to me.'

'And where does religion come into it?'

'Religion tells us that the creator God is jealous and vengeful and if we don't believe the right things he'll consign us to eternal damnation. All religions believe that they have the right beliefs which by definition make all the others wrong. In the past religious people executed people who didn't believe what the Church taught. They massacred each other in war, for no other reason than that they didn't believe the right thing and all in the name of a loving God. It doesn't make sense and that's one of the reasons I left.'

'What were the others?'

'If there were an all-powerful, all-loving God why would he allow earthquakes that kill thousands of people and make hundreds of thousands of people homeless and consigned to live the rest of their lives in refugee camps in total misery? This doesn't make sense to me either. I believe and accept that earthquakes happen because of the natural phenomenon of the movement of tectonic plates and there is nothing we can do about it. If you believe in a God you need to answer the question as to why such a God allows babies to be born with cancer and appalling deformities, why does he not intervene to prevent millions of people every year from dying of starvation and all the other appalling evils in this world. That it's all our fault or that he'll sort it all out at a last judgment is a pathetic attempt to duck these questions.

'To me science and reason make sense and theology and faith don't. That's why I left and I have been contented with myself ever since. The thing that puzzles me most is that there are better-read people with better minds than mine in the Church who go on believing and if they have these kinds of question they don't appear to take them seriously.'

'Some people believe that you can reconcile science and religion.'

'Well it's as simple as this. I don't.'

I had never put all this together for Kate before. She had accepted me on trust because she loved me and I loved her. As for many people these things weren't an issue; they didn't bother her.

'Is there anything you miss about religion since you left?'

'I did value then being part of a community and I valued the Eucharist as a ritual, despite the fact I believed that it wasn't what the Church claimed it to be. It's well known that those things which formerly religious people miss when they become atheist are community and ritual.'

'Do you ever regret that you left?'

'No, I have no regrets whatever; nowadays I don't feel the need for community or for ritual in my life. Don't misunderstand me, I haven't by any means all the answers. Not even religion claims that. What I have is an easy mind and a clear conscience. I'm happy where I am. I'm not constantly struggling to reconcile religion to the reality of the world around me. I believe that the most important thing for anybody to do and for us to teach our children is to think for oneself. That's what I do rightly or wrongly. I'll go down to the grave or up to the crematorium with a clear conscience. I'll have done the best I can to make sense of the whole thing. Everybody has to make up their own mind and we all do it in our own way. Some abdicate their beliefs to religious institutions and their teachings, some make up their own minds and some don't address the matter at all.'

'I liked that pastor this morning,' said Kate. 'There was something honest about him. I didn't agree with everything he said, but he really wanted everybody else to have what he had and I was probably the only person there that didn't have it.'

CHAPTER 5

A domestic routine had settled upon each of us. Siobhán's annual school reports were good. 'Conscientious' and 'works well' were words that teachers used in their comments. What pleased Kate as much as these were comments by her form teacher under 'Conduct' like 'helpful' and 'good'. It became clear that in the science/arts divide Siobhán was on the science side.

She had become more amenable to the rhythm of the home and contributed in her own way to chores that had to be done. She had her moments, but on the whole she had become more pleasant to live with. From time to time she surprised us by being thoughtful or helpful beyond what we had come to expect. She and Kate, without it becoming an issue, had worked out in practice a way of accommodating each other that made for harmony most of the time. From this I benefited too. In Siobhán's teenage years, when their relationship had been fraught, I had never taken sides and Kate had never expected that I would. Now Siobhán came to treat me courteously, and sometimes even warmly. Occasionally she would ask me a question about the Bible, religion or belief as though she genuinely wanted to know, rather than that she wanted to hold up her own evangelical beliefs over against conventional Church doctrine or over against my non-belief.

She was growing into an attractive young woman, but Kate and I both felt there was something unresolved within her. We didn't know if Siobhán was aware that this was so and if she did, what it might be. We both felt that the issue might be that her father had deserted her. She never talked about him or asked her mother questions. She was too young to remember him and he hadn't even asked Kate about her when she was in communication with him on matters concerning their separation. We were pretty certain that if this was the issue she was far more likely to discuss it with Judy than with Kate. Her relationship with Judy was as firm as ever, and Kate comforted herself that Judy was a soul mate with whom Siobhán could discuss things that she might find it hard to discuss with her mother.

Kate was now in a permanent teaching position that suited her well and her colleagues were congenial. I had an undemanding job that I anticipated I would have until it was time to retire. I had a wage from which I contributed my share to the household budget and had enough left over for my needs – mainly books.

In my former life I had worked on my own with people most of whom had set me apart to one extent or another. I had had to cope with all kinds of people; those who, as they would put it, had respect for my office to those who were deferential and obsequious: the helpful, the awkward, the enthusiastic, the apathetic, the communicative, the silent, the educated, the uneducated, employers, employees, fathers, mothers, children; in summary, every sort and condition of man, woman and child that you can imagine. I knew them in their homes and in many cases I knew the inside stories of their lives insofar as they wanted to reveal them to me, and for many I had been involved with them in their problems, in their sorrows and in their joys. In the early years I found my life fulfilling working with people, but sometimes I found it wearying and had to develop a distance in order to survive. For so many years all of this had been complicated by Jennifer's drinking that had almost dragged me down to a point that I hadn't been able to function.

In my new life I was a small contributor to the world of commerce. I worked from eight o'clock in the morning until five o'clock in the evening five days a week. During that time I lived in a world that was a hundred miles away from the world I had lived in formerly. This was a world almost entirely of men; store men, packers, truck drivers. Nobody made unreasonable demands on me but on the other hand I had none of the satisfactions of my former life. Nobody expected more of me than that I do my job. Most of the men I worked with, and the drivers that came and went, were working people. Most of them had the same kinds of interests; football, horses, gossip, scandals. Most of them had a human decency uncontaminated by wealth, status or ambition. Not that they didn't indulge fantasies about winning the lottery and how they would spend it. They read the same kinds of tabloid newspapers and without exception drank pints of stout with great regularity. In the warehouse there was an ethos of camaraderie and banter and most of them had that male propensity to provoke a rise out of each other. I knew almost nothing about the families of my work colleagues and nothing at all about the drivers who came and went. The work was undemanding and had a beginning and an end. The working day went quickly and week-ends were my own. The men I worked with knew where I had come from and what I had been and it wasn't an issue. They accepted me as I was and I knew I had been accepted when they started to make jokes about my former life as what they called a 'sky pilot'. Most of them addressed me as 'Reverend' or 'Rev' and some didn't use any name or title. At first I tried to make sure they called me 'John' but soon gave up. On Fridays after work I would go with them to the pub, have one pint and go home. They accepted that my Friday ritual was different from theirs. They were comfortable with that and so was I.

When we came to the city Kate and I had looked forward to going to theatre and the Concert Hall more often. We did for a while, but then we became lazy about going out at night, especially in the winter. We tried not to vegetate and forced ourselves to have a good walk three or four times a week. Our Sunday morning walk by the sea became our weekly ritual when we communed with each other and the universe.

One weekend a friend of Kate's from where we had lived in the country, gave her some surprising news. Kate knew that the mother of Betty, the woman with whom Conor had eloped, had died. She had been a former parishioner of mine. This event ran entirely contrary to the woman's well laid plans. Everything Betty's mother did and planned was predicated on the assumption that, as she was quite a bit younger than him, she would survive her husband and have total control of everything, especially the farm. She would run things her way. This plan would not under any circumstance include Betty, whom she believed to have disgraced the family by running away with a married man. Having by the necessity of her premature death foregone any say in the matter her husband, who had always been ready to receive back and forgive Betty, invited his daughter home to take on the farm.

When word spread locally that Betty was coming home rumour was rife. Rumour had it that Betty, known to be an able farmer, would run the farm and Conor would set up his architect practice again; both would run the farm; they were coming home to look after the old man and the farm would be let; they were coming home to farm and Betty's father would be going into a nursing home. As is the case with gossip in small communities there was any combination of these and of anything else that entered the heads of people. However the one thing that nobody had rumoured transpired. To the surprise of everybody Betty came home on her own to farm and look after her father. This gave rise to the belief that, as Betty's father was in poor health, Betty would stay until he died, sell up and return to Canada.

One evening at dinner Kate said to Siobhán:

'I was talking to Jean on the phone today. She tells me that Betty, who went to Canada with your father, is home to run the family farm. She isn't going back.'

'What are you saying?'

'I'll go,' I said.

'No stay, it's all right with me,' said Siobhán.

'According to Jean they've separated. Your father is staying in Canada.'

'Mum, would you ever call him Conor. That's his name. I'm an adult now. "Your father" makes him sound like a function. You don't call him "my husband".'

'Conor is staying in Canada.'

'It's funny you should bring this up now. Judy asked me recently if I remember him. I have no memory of him whatever since I was less than two years old when he left. Judy wanted to know if I had any wish to meet him.'

'And have you?'

'Of course I have. I'm his flesh and blood and he's mine. That he left was between you and him, but he's still my father. You never talked to me about him.'

'I felt that was your prerogative to bring it up, but you never did.'

Siobhán stood up, went around the table and hugging Kate said:

'Mum, thank you for everything you've done for me, but I'd still like to meet my Dad.'

Kate overcome with emotion could not reply. She stood up and the two hugged tightly.

'It's strange that we are only talking about this now, but what kind of a man was he?'

'You've seen photos of him, some with you in them.'

'I want to hear it from you, and not just what he looked like.'

'Well I'll tell you that first. Physically he was a couple of inches taller than I am. He had a fine head of dark brown hair, which you have inherited, tinged with a reddish hue from me. He was well built – strong. He had a good sense of humour. I never heard him tell a joke and he wasn't impressed by jokes that other people told, but he was quick to see humour in human situations; in what people said and did. He was good fun. He was generous. I was devastated when he went.'

'What happened? Why did he leave?'

'I had no hint of it at the time, and the only thing he ever said was in a letter a few years after he had gone when we were negotiating a settlement. He said simply. "I had fallen out of love with you." These things happen. It seems that falling in and out of love just happen. There's no accounting for them. He left with Betty, so presumably he had fallen in love with her. The great mystery to me is how he could have left you. He adored you.'

'It's simple,' said Siobhán, 'falling in love doesn't include children. It's about making children, but it doesn't usually include existing ones,' and turning to me Siobhán asked:

'And when did you come on the scene?'

'As you know Jennifer was a friend of your Mum. She was a bad alcoholic and Kate was the only person I could talk to about it. She was a great help to me when I was at my wits' end coping with Jennifer's drinking. Then Jennifer had an accident and died, and in a little while Kate and I came together.'

'That was handy.'

'Well it was really,' I said, 'we knew each other very well; Kate was getting over her loss and I was getting over mine. I had helped her when Conor left and she helped me when Jennifer was in a bad way. Then it just happened.'

'As you say, these things just happen, like Judy and me.'

'Why don't you write to Conor and you and Judy go to Canada to see him after the Leaving? A reward for how hard you've worked.'

'Are you serious?'

'Of course I'm serious. I wouldn't make a suggestion like that if I weren't.'

'I'll think about it, Mum, and I'll talk to Judy.'

Judy was delighted with the idea, so Siobhán wrote to her father. After a week or so there was great anticipation for the arrival of the post. A week passed, two weeks, three and then a month. Siobhán's exams were looming and Kate was sorry she hadn't waited to talk to Siobhán about her father until after the exams were over. A few days before her first paper a letter with a Toronto postmark addressed to Siobhán, arrived. She was about to leave for school. She read the letter, threw it on the kitchen table and said: 'read it' and left. Kate read the letter to me:

My dear Siobhán,

What a wonderful surprise it was to me to receive your letter. I don't deserve that you should have made contact with me. I have lived for the past fifteen or sixteen years with the guilt that I deserted you. I could too easily say that a day didn't pass that I didn't think of you.

That would not be true. However, I thought of you often, and over the years when I saw young girls that I calculated were about your age I wondered how you looked and were you happy. I had no right to know.

It would be a wonderful thrill for me if you and your friend Judy were to come to Toronto. There is plenty of room in the house; just let me know dates so that I can arrange to take time off work to spend with you and show you around.

Good luck with the Leaving, and I look forward to hearing from you.

Love, Conor

P.S. Sorry for the delay in replying; I have been very busy at work.

Kate handed the letter to me: 'I'm glad that's the way it has worked out; it'd be a blow for her at the beginning of the Leaving if it hadn't. I had no idea how he might react.'

'Is this the Conor you knew?' I asked.

'It is really. He was honourable in a selfish kind of way.'

CHAPTER 6

As so often happens, even in the worst of summers, when the Leaving exams start there is a spell of fine, warm, sunny weather. Siobhán and Judy like thousands of others, who for months had worked all the hours of the clock, were incarcerated in a silent exam hall to do their best to impress and even to outwit their examiners instead of enjoying the early summer sun. Parents sweated powerlessly in the hope that their children would do well and avoid the disappointment of failing to make the course on which they had set their hearts. Siobhán and Judy had both worked hard and often studied together. Until the time came that she had had to decide Kate had no idea what Siobhán was likely to do. It was clear that she would go to third level, but when Kate broached the subject it was always a case of:

'I'm really not sure what I want to do.'

When finally she had to make up her mind she announced that she would be a nurse. I was surprised and asked Kate if she were surprised too.

'Yes, in a way. She never said anything, but when she was small she always talked to her dolls in a caring way. They were often sick and she would look after them. She was always good with old people too. I've only put that together since she told us. I hope she's making the right decision.'

Judy, who was particularly bright, had always wanted to be a doctor. Her first choice was medicine and it was likely she would get the points she needed.

Siobhán slogged her way through the exams and after each paper she gave us an account of how she thought she had done.

For example on the evening of her English paper she said:

'I'll get about 60 per cent, but why people think so much of poets and why they can't say what they want to say in plain English I have no idea. They're determined to confound anyone that is weird enough to read their poems. I can assure you that I've read the last poem I'll ever have anything to do with.'

When Siobhán had finished her last exam the tension in the house dissipated. She was excited at the prospect of going to Canada to meet her father. One evening a couple of weeks before they were due to go Siobhán said:

'What if we don't get on? We mightn't like each other.'

'It's hard to believe that you won't get on with the man who wrote that letter to you,' I said, thinking it was easier in the circumstances for me to comment rather than Kate. I had met Conor only a few times before he had gone away with Betty and it was a mystery to me how he could have deserted his beautiful little daughter and such a wonderful woman as Kate. We were glad that Judy would be with her. Judy was a firm friend to Siobhán and had a wise head beyond her years. Her influence had steadied the ship when Siobhán had been in turbulent waters and their religious belief would stand them in good stead.

Siobhán knew that the weather in a Canadian summer could be pretty hot, so Kate took her into town one Saturday morning to shop. She wanted one formal outfit:

'He might bring us out to dinner or have some of his friends in to meet us; I don't want to let him down.'

A few days before she was due to go Siobhán decided it was time to pack. During this fraught procedure she consulted Kate a number of times.

'She's nervous, and she's not under any illusions. She wondered sarcastically if she were to meet some of his friends would he introduce her as "this is my daughter Siobhán. I abandoned her when she was two," and laughed.'

'I can understand him leaving,' Siobhán had said, 'but never having been in touch. Why didn't he write to me when he knew I was old enough to understand these things?'

'Ask him when you get there, but not for a few days. Wait and see how you both get on.' Kate had counselled.

We both went to the airport to see them off. Siobhán was quiet and as they left us and went towards security Judy put her arm around Siobhán's shoulder. Kate too was upset and cried as we went back to the car.

'I'm crying for Siobhán. I hope she isn't disappointed.'

After about a week we had a post card from them. They gave no indication whatever of how things were. Four or five days later a letter arrived:

Dear Mum and John,

The flight was fine. We didn't talk much about meeting Conor until the pilot announced that we were starting our approach to Toronto. Judy took my hand and squeezed it gently. I burst into tears and was sorry that we'd come. Judy as usual reassured me: 'don't cross bridges before you come to them.' We said a prayer together and I felt better.

'At passport control an immigration woman took us aside to a small room and questioned us: the purpose of our visit, who we would be staying with and for how long. 'Is your father a Canadian citizen?' I told her I didn't know. When had I stayed with him last? And I had to admit I never had. Then Judy in about three or four sentences gave her a summary of the situation and the woman's attitude changed.

She smiled warmly and said: 'Good luck. Off you go.' I'll never forget her. She was kind.

In the arrivals area we immediately saw Conor. He stood holding a sign 'Siobhán and Judy.' Judy said quietly to me: 'go ahead'. He hugged me tightly and held me for a long time. I cried and Conor's eyes filled up. He kissed Judy on the cheek and said: 'I've been looking forward to you both coming. I've been nervous about it but now I'm relieved to see you.'

As we went to the car park he told us where he lived, the kind of neighbourhood it was, how far from down-town and pointed out things of interest on the way. His house was a typical Canadian four bedroom sub-urban house with a large basement in an upper-middle-class suburb. He was very good; as he said in his letter he took time off from work to show us around. On the morning after we arrived he took us to Niagara Falls, the following morning he dropped us down-town and met us in the afternoon. On the way back to the house he told us that a friend of his Geraldine, was coming in the evening and they were taking us out to dinner to a favourite restaurant of theirs.

Geraldine arrived and immediately the same thing struck both of us: how like you, Mum, she was. Same type, short, round face, but nothing like you in temperament. She was brash, knew everything there was to know about Conor and wanted to let us know she did. She knew the workings of the house and we were both sure that she was living with him, but had moved out for the duration of our stay. She worked in the same office as Conor. We didn't like her. She brought us one day to an old Indian longhouse north of the city. It was interesting and again she knew all about it. She knew more than the guide.

On the Sunday we went to a local church. Conor stayed in bed and it was clear that, like you and John, he never went anywhere. Later in the day he asked us about what we believed and we told him. He was surprised. We told him that you came with us occasionally. He asked us about boyfriends; Judy caught my eye and gave me one of her wicked winks. Mum, I have to tell you he didn't ask about you at all. He only mentioned you once. We did; we talked about you and how happy you and John are together. He didn't respond. He didn't even say 'that's good' or 'I'm glad to hear it.' He said nothing. The only mention he made was one day he said that he left because there was nothing any longer between you. That was it. You were one up on Betty though; he didn't mention her at all!

One day in the car out of the blue Judy asked him: 'did you miss Siobhán when you left?

'Of course I did but the place for a little girl of that age is with her mother.' She had a sense that he wouldn't say more and she didn't pursue it.

I'm glad I came. It has laid a ghost and answered a lot of questions for me, but I wouldn't want to come again.

We look forward to seeing you both on Saturday. All the news then.

Lots of love,

Siobhán and Judy xx oo

We were relieved that Siobhán was glad she had gone. It was ideal that Judy had been with her. Kate could not and would not have gone with her and it would not have been right for her to have gone on her own. That her visit had 'laid a ghost and answered a lot of questions' could only have been good, and the two had had what sounded like a good holiday in Canada to boot.

We met them at the airport. They were both all smiles. Siobhán ran forward and hugged and hugged Kate. They held each other without a word spoken or necessary. After kisses all round we made for the car-park.

'I told you the important parts in the letter, but I'll tell you the fine detail when we're home.'

We dropped Judy home first and it was clear that she too was delighted with their visit to Canada. Siobhán gave us little bits of information about their time with Conor but it was late:

'I have some photos to show you in the morning.' She was tired, had something to eat and we went to bed.

In the morning Siobhán didn't waken until almost noon. When she arrived downstairs she had her photos. Siobhán gave us an illustrated chronological account of their holiday.

'He's balder and fatter than when he went away,' Kate commented.

'Maybe that's why Betty left him,' Siobhán replied.

'I can't wait to see this woman who looks like me.' Kate said with great good humour.

Holding a photo with the back facing Kate, Siobhán did a 'dan de dan dan' and turned it around.

'Good grief she's not like me. John, stand up for me. She isn't like me.'

'Well she's your build and has the same shape face,' I said.

'That's what I said; same type,' Siobhán said.

'That's what you often hear,' I said, 'a man's wife dies after a long marriage and he takes up with a woman of the same type or even a dollybird that his friends swear is uncannily like his wife was at that age.'

'That's the way we're programmed,' I said.

'But I'm not a bit like Jennifer was.'

'No, but I found the switch to the programme and flipped it. That's the story of my life: do it your own way.'

Siobhán was highly amused at this conversation, finished showing us the photos and went to have some breakfast.

I was the one that had to work during the summer. Kate and Siobhán were free from the end of June until September and I had my two week holiday from work. Kate and I went to Cork to see her family. Her brother, Eamon, was in the home place and milked a herd of Friesians. Her two sisters, both married with families, lived in the area. I knew them all and they knew the story of Kate and me. We were well received and there was no awkwardness despite the fact that they were all traditional mass-going Catholics. Like many older people it was simply a case that that was the way they were brought up and they didn't question it. If they did give it a thought they didn't say so.

One morning I went with Eamon in the Jeep to an out-farm to herd. We weren't out of the yard when Eamon said:

'You know John that Margaret and I both go to mass. The youngsters come sometimes when they're home just to please their mother, but I know they don't go when they're away. For both of us it's a habit of a lifetime, but from time to time I think about it and you know, I don't believe the half it.' It didn't surprise me; Eamon was a highly intelligent and reflective man.

'I think,' I said, 'there are a lot of people in your position who find the doctrines incredible but value religion for community; somewhere to go to meet other people, something to help people to come together. For people who think about the world, the universe, life and death, it helps them do something about the mystery. Some people don't think about it at all and accept the whole thing on trust from the Church that claims to have all the answers. The young people have been taught to think for themselves and most of them quietly leave religion aside and live their lives.'

'You're right,' said Eamon, 'and the thing is that there is a lot of integrity and goodness amongst the youngsters and they have it without believing all the stuff.'

'There are no simple answers to the big questions.' I said. 'The best we can do is try to help each other through life as best we can, and there are a lot of people to whom life has dealt a rotten hand and who need a lot of help. You don't need to believe in three persons in one God to do that. In fact some of the finest people who work for humanitarian causes don't believe in a God at all.'

There was a long silence. Then Eamon asked:

'What do you make of this life-after-death business? I have the impression that you don't believe it.'

'No I don't.'

'Well to tell you the truth, neither do I.'

'As I see it, Eamon, it's a human aspiration to do with fear of death, fear of the unknown, and the Church uses this fear as an instrument to frighten the wits out of people so they'll toe the line. "Believe what we tell you and do what we say and we'll get you there and if you don't you'll end up in the other place. We have the true way of doing this so all the others who tell you that they have it right are wrong."'

Eamon was interested so I went on:

'It makes more sense to me that when you're dead you're dead and you'll always be dead, and that doesn't frighten me at all. However, I probably won't be too keen to face it when the time comes. There are some wonderful things to explore in this life, but on balance it's a rotten bloody world of evil, pain and suffering. In two world wars the best part of ninety million people were killed and goodness knows how many wounded, and there are always wars throughout the world. Then there has been ethnic cleansing; the holocaust, Bosnia and Rwanda, famines, earthquakes and tsunamis, lies, greed, corruption, bitterness and hatred between nations, peoples and families and much, much more. There is of course too truth and beauty, love, kindness and heroic altruism. If it were possible to quantify these two categories what would the proportions be? Eighty percent evil, 20 percent good, or even ninety percent evil, ten percent good. For millions and millions of people it's a terrible bloody world through no fault of their own. There are fates worse than death and millions of people as we speak are enduring them.'

I told Eamon some of my experience in which I thought he might find something to relate to without putting him on the spot:

'The simple truth is that you don't know what people believe unless they tell you. You may think you know from odd bits and pieces a person says or from how they behave, but unless they tell you outright it's only speculation. In parishes it was rare that anyone would tell me what they believed. We assume that people believe what they were taught as children, what the Church teaches. Most do, but this is not the case for some people who are churchgoers and are involved in their parish.

'People stand up in church on Sunday and solemnly recite the creed without knowing what precisely it is they are affirming. As time went on I myself used to leave out phrases of the creed that I simply did not believe; for example: "I believe in the communion of saints" because I didn't. Eventually I was skipping so many phrases that I would start them off and stand mute for the rest. An intelligent parishioner who went to church every Sunday once told me that that he never said the creed because he didn't understand much of it and didn't believe the bits he did understand.' Eamon asked the obvious question:

'Why did he go to church then?'

'I didn't ask him, but I believe it was for community and a deep down need for ritual in the face of the mystery of life and of the universe. A way of addressing this mystery and saying: "In the culture in which I was brought up this is the best I know how."'

'That's what I feel,' said Eamon, 'I don't believe a lot of it, but I think I'd miss it if I didn't go. Do you go at all?'

'No, I don't.' I said, 'I haven't been to church for a long, long time. I don't miss it, and Kate says that's probably because I had an overdose of it over the years in the job, enough to do me a couple of lifetimes. I'm sure that's part of it, but when I go to a wedding or funeral I'm reminded of how much I no longer believe. When I finally admitted to myself that I didn't believe there was a God I began to see everything from a new perspective, and from this perspective when I'm at a baptism, wedding or funeral I am reminded how incredulous I am at what the Church teaches and what people believe.'

'Kate told me recently that she doesn't go either,' said Eamon.

'No, but she sometimes has a niggling feeling that there might be something in it. Having been brought up Catholic at a time in Ireland when the Catholic Church was triumphant, it was better at indoctrinating children than the kind of Protestantism I was brought up in. Much of what children absorb in those early years of values, attitudes and beliefs is indelible and hard to kick. Not only that, but Catholic indoctrination was heavily laced with guilt, and a residue of unreasonable guilt rears its ugly head from time to time in the adult's life and creates this niggling doubt that it just might be true.' Eamon seemed to me to be taking all of this in so I went on:

'In case you think that's all Protestant prejudice, there's a brand of evangelical Protestantism that is good at the indoctrination and guilt business too. They too frighten the wits out of people with the threat of hell to get them on board and to keep them there. In my experience, people who are brought up in this kind of evangelical Protestantism are the same as Catholics; they can never kick the habit completely for fear it just might be true.'

'I'm a bit like that,' said Eamon. 'I'm hedging my bets in case it turns out to be true.'

We arrived at the out-farm, left the Jeep at the side of the road and went into a field. In this field of the finest grass there was a herd of store cattle Eamon was fattening. His expert eye took in every one of them as we crossed the field towards them. They all looked alike to me, but Eamon was keeping an eye for one in particular that he had had a doubt about when had herded the previous day. He found it, stood still to watch it move and still wasn't sure.

'I'll have to bring him home later and dose him and if that doesn't do the trick I'll get the vet to take a look at him; I think there's something wrong.' He counted them and we went back to the Jeep.

'Wouldn't it be great to have as little to worry about as those ones,' Eamon said, 'eat and sleep without a worry in the world until the time comes and then not to know a thing about it. If there is a God could he not have organised things so that we didn't have to kill other animals to live.'

'We don't have to. We could all be vegetarians,' I said.

'What about wild animals? A lot of them kill other animals to live, and the ones they kill are often vegetarian. Even a fella with a modicum of intelligence could have arranged things better to avoid fear and suffering. Anyway since that's the way things are and, God or no God, we have to put up with it.'

'As you know Kate doesn't eat meat or fish,' I said.

'That doesn't surprise me. When Kate was growing up she had a mind of her own. It was never as simple as doing what she was told. I can hear my father saying to her in exasperation: "That's the why. Do what you're told." She had to know 'why' and more often than not she had an opinion of her own or another question to ask.'

'That's the way she still is, but she doesn't trumpet her opinions,' I said.

'I remember well, I was in the car with her when my father was driving her to the bus the day she was going to Dublin to her first job. My father said:

'You know that the most important thing you can teach those children is to know right from wrong. "No Daddy," she said, "the most important thing I can teach those children is to think for themselves and if they can do that everything else falls into place." That stuck in my mind; I've never forgotten it.'

'That's Kate all right. She never lost it,' I assured him.

While we were in Cork Judy had come to stay with Siobhán. They were plugging in the time waiting for their Leaving results. If they achieved the points they wanted they would both be offered their first choice, nursing and medicine. If they fell short they were both determined to sit the Leaving again to make the points they needed. If either didn't make it, it was likely to be Siobhán. Judy was particularly bright; Siobhán was bright enough and had worked hard.

I hadn't many more years left before I received the State pension, when I would no longer have to be up every week-day morning to check containers. While the work itself was tedious, I would miss the lads in the warehouse and the drivers. I enjoyed their innate sense of how to make something of life – the good bits and the bad. As a general rule they had a decency and human empathy that seemed to me to diminish for most people the better off they were and the further up the social ladder. The men at work had no unreal aspirations and largely they were content with their lot, but all of them had plans of what they would do when they won the lottery! The prospect gave them an opportunity to indulge a weekly fantasy. Something to hope for that would lift them out of the tedium of their routine. To my surprise not all of them said they would give up work. Early on, at a lunch break, one of them asked me why I didn't buy lottery tickets:

'Because I'm not interested in winning it. It would destroy me if I won it.'

'You could give it away.'

'To us,' one of the young fellows chipped in with a laugh.

'You could give it to charity.'

'I could. I could give some of it to my family, but money doesn't contribute one whit to making us happy. We think it does but that's an illusion.' This opinion confirmed them in their view that I was odd or entirely mad. I had no idea what they thought of this, but whatever they thought they didn't let it affect them.

One day at lunch break one of them said:

'Did you see that programme on TV about the private lives of footballers?'

'Yea, they don't know what to do with their money.'

'I didn't see it,' I said, 'the trouble is these guys leave school early and apart from football they haven't anything to interest them in their spare time.'

'What do you watch on TV?' one of them asked.

'Current affairs,' I said, 'but I'm fed up with all those absurd politicians saying things solely to promote themselves and designed to get themselves re-elected.'

'Those fellas'd give me a pain in the arse.' One of them gave this succinct, if uneducated, summary of what I had said.

'What I really enjoy,' I went on, 'is ballet.' I had long ago decided not to trim my sails to accommodate their opinion of me.

'Jesus,' one of them exclaimed, and there was silence. Then one of them said:

'Did ye ever think o' keepin' pigeons?'

Despite everything they took me as I was. They were aware that I was different but treated me the same as they treated each other and to be accepted by them in this way meant a lot to me.

When I worked as a clergyman in a parish it had given me access to people to be of some use. Now I didn't have that. In one parish I had gone around in my mind all the families on the parish list and found that every one of them, without exception, was currently coping with a problem of some kind, acute or chronic, family, personal, children, health, bereavement or had coped with a problem within the past couple of years. This included the rectory family. Nobody escapes. In most families there aren't many periods of 'plain sailing'. Life is an adventure punctuated by problems and difficulties and even tragedies, and there's no accounting for why some people 'get it in the neck' more than others. Parishioners in difficulty often turn to the rector as somebody they feel they can trust. Somebody they can talk to in confidence:

'Rector, my boy Tom is only seventeen and he's out at night drinking and arriving home in the small hours. We can't get him up in the morning to help his father with the jobs. He won't do a thing we tell him; we've tried everything but he won't listen to us. He's gone wild. If you'd come out and talk to him he'd listen to you.'

How deluded can people be? Do they think that the rector is more in touch with God and that Tom will take notice of God? The rector is Jack of all trades and master of none, and can only help with moral support. Ordination doesn't confer the gift to solve people's problems, so the best one can do is to be supportive and encourage people to find the right professional help. Some clergy are good at this and some are hopeless, but none by reason of their office has the inside track. I had been a provider of moral support and found it satisfying to be able to help in that way. Since I left I wasn't doing anything for other people and my life was self-centred with one exception. The fellows at work, even one or two of the drivers, occasionally spoke to me about their problems. They all knew my background, and that I had left it, so they couldn't have thought that I had some special influence. I was able to listen and that in itself was a help. When I came to retire I would miss even this little bit of usefulness. I wouldn't miss the tedium, but I'd miss the company.

Kate and I returned from Cork with less than two weeks to wait for Siobhán's Leaving results. As the day came closer the tension in the house increased. On the morning the results were due when Siobhán heard the sound of the post-box flap she ran into the hall. Kate and I froze at the breakfast table. There was thirty seconds of unbearable unknowing and then a shout from the hall: 'yipee, yipee'. Siobhán rushed into the kitchen:

'I've more than enough, more than enough.' She put the envelope and sheet on the table in front of Kate and rushed back to the hall to phone Judy. Her post hadn't arrived yet. There were more 'yipees' as Siobhán came back and danced around the kitchen. There was no word from Judy for the best part of an hour. Then the phone rang. Siobhán answered. There was an ominous silence. We heard Siobhán say:

'But you'll still be able to do medicine.'

That's what transpired: they were offered places at the two different universities in the city. At first they were disappointed, but soon became reconciled to the fact that they wouldn't be together as they had expected.

CHAPTER 7

One Saturday morning, shortly after Siobhán had started university, I wasn't long back from the shops with the croissants and newspaper. Siobhán was still in bed and Kate and I were having our usual late breakfast at the kitchen table when the doorbell rang. Kate answered it and came back.

'There's a man and woman and child at the door for you.'

'Who are they?'

'I have no idea. I didn't enquire. They asked for you by name and used "Reverend"'. I put down the paper, sure in my mind it was a former parishioner or someone sent by a former parishioner that thought I might be able to help in some way. I went to the door and there stood a man who was vaguely familiar and a woman and young boy I didn't recognise.

'Hello,' the man said, and put out his hand. I shook his hand without knowing who he was.

'I'm over visiting my mother's family and thought I'd call. This is my wife Barbara and our son Billy.' At this I tumbled to it; this was John who had called to me in the country not long before Jennifer died saying that he was my son by a woman I had been in love with who had worked with me in the bank. She had gone to England and I had gone on to study for ordination. In the circumstances that he had recounted to me, not only was it perfectly possible, but I had accepted that I was his father. He was my son with Maura

Murray who before she died in her early fifties had recounted our relationship to him. As Jennifer was in the depths of her decent into the maelstrom of her enslavement to alcohol at the time I didn't follow it up. He had written to me subsequently saying he was on hard times and asking me to lend him money. He phoned later on but Jennifer was seriously ill in hospital at the time and I couldn't do anything for him. There had been no further contact between us until now.

I had told Kate all of this but hadn't told my children, Mary and Peter, about their older half brother. Nor did Siobhán know about him.

I brought them into the sitting-room and went to the kitchen and told Kate who they were and she came to meet them. She offered tea or coffee and went back to the kitchen.

'How have you been keeping?' John asked. I told him I was fine and that I would be retiring in a few years.

'Eventually I trained as an electrician,' he said, 'I married Barbara and we have this little bundle of energy.'

'What's your name?' I asked the boy. He turned away and buried his face in his mother's lap.

'This is Billy,' she said.

Kate came in with a tray and a picture book for the little fellow and left.

'I haven't been to Ireland for a long time' John said, 'we're over to see my mother's family. I was going through a bad time the last time I was in touch with you.'

'I'm sorry I wasn't able to help. My wife was in hospital and died a short time after that. It was a difficult time for me too. As I'm sure you know since you have found me, I'm no longer in the ministry. Life's like that,' I said, 'everybody goes through difficult times and some come through and unfortunately some don't.'

'Barbara turned my life around and Billy has crowned it.' Barbara demurred with an embarrassed smile.

As we talked on it brought back to me those early years in the bank. I remembered my life consumed by my love for Maura and hers for me. Not only was I in love with her, but I admired her and had had an immense respect for her; she had been a practising Catholic, but with a mind of her own. In our first conversation in the rectory John had told me that knowing she was pregnant and that I was considering ordination, she went to England not to make things difficult for me. I did not regret my time in the ministry and I did not regret leaving. I did however, when I learned of it, regret that Maura had had to cope on her own. It appeared that it worked out well for her in the end. She had brought up John, and by his account she had had a good marriage, but giving birth and making a life for herself and her baby at the start must have been difficult.

I went to the kitchen to ask Kate to come in again. After the best part of an hour John said:

'We'd better go. I just wanted Barbara to meet you and Billy to meet his granddad.' We stood up and I picked up my only grandchild. He didn't resist, but turned toward his mother and put out his hand. I gave him to her and realised that I had no right to any other response from him. John and I averred that we would stay in touch.

I was glad they had called. It had completed significant business that had been left in the air since he was last in touch. I was particularly glad to learn that John, like his mother, had managed to make a life for himself.

Now I would have to tell my children; Mary, who was married and had no children, and Peter who lived with Tony, his partner. I felt that Peter would have no problem, but I wasn't sure how Mary would take it. I had no doubt that I should tell them separately. I would want to have told Peter first to be able to tell Mary that he had taken it well, but I knew in that circumstance she would almost certainly stand on her dignity as the older and expect that she should have been told first.

I talked it over with Kate. We decided two things. Firstly that I should invite Mary to our house to tell her so that she could decide whether and when to tell her husband Tom. Secondly, I should not tell Siobhán until I had told Mary and Peter.

I phoned Mary and asked her to call one evening:

'There's something I want to talk to you about.'

'What is it?'

'I don't want to talk about it on the phone.'

'You're being very mysterious.'

'Not really. Come one evening; it isn't urgent.'

'You've made me curious. I'll come tomorrow evening.'

I rehearsed different kinds of openings to present the facts to her, but found there was little I could do about how I told her that might make it easier for her to accept. I didn't want to injure my relationship with her, but at this stage of my life I had no difficulty with the whole circumstance of John, and I had no control over whether she would accept it or not.

The following evening we sat together in the sitting-room.

'What's the great mystery?' Mary began.

'There's no mystery. You know that after I left school I worked in a bank for a few years before I went to college to train for ordination ….' and I told her the story right up until John's recent visit with his wife and son. She did not interrupt, and when I had finished she said:

'Who else knows?'

'Kate is the only one.'

'Did Mum know?'

'No. When John turned up she was so deep into her alcoholism there was no point in telling her. Had she recovered I would have told her. I am certain that she would have accepted it and even have admired Maura for what she had done.'

'I bet she went to England not to spare you but to hide it from her family. Why didn't she tell you? You were the father. Did she not have to have your permission if she gave your name for his birth certificate? Or did she put for Father's Name? "Don't know", "Irish Army" or some such.'

'John told me his mother told him she did as she did so as not to interfere with my plan to be ordained, and that fits with the Maura Murray I knew. There's no point in going into all that now; it's water under the bridge.'

'What do you want me to do?'

'Nothing. I just want you to know.'

'Well now I do. I needn't tell you it's a surprise but it's really none of my business.'

'Unless you consider that having a half-brother is your business.'

'I don't want to meet him.'

'You don't have to. I simply thought I owed it to you to tell you.'

'Are you going to tell Peter?'

'Of course I am. He's coming tomorrow evening.'

'Are you going to tell Siobhán?'

'Yes, after I've told Peter.'

'She'll pray for you.' That was unfair, but I let it pass. 'Well, if you've no more surprises I'd better go. Tom will be curious about what the mystery is.' Mary left without giving me her usual kiss on the cheek. I was disappointed; I wouldn't want it to lead to estrangement between us, but I had to allow for what a revelation it was for her and that she had a right to be at least surprised.

Peter was a different kettle of fish:

'Dad, weren't you the boyo. Tony won't be a bit surprised. As I've told you before, he has a great admiration for your ability to be your own person, to make your own decisions, not that that was a decision you made on your own. As they say: "It takes two to tango." How's the job? Are you not bored stiff checking those containers?'

'Of course I am, but it's relieved by the lads I work with. They're good company and they live in a real world that I know nothing about. Anyway I haven't long to go now.'

'What will you do with your time?'

'I've loads of reading to catch up with. How anybody who can read is bored is beyond me.'

In the hall on his way out Peter said:

'If John is over again tell him I'd like to meet him; there are a few things I'd like to tell him about his father.' I laughed. 'I'm serious; I'd like to meet him,' and he was gone.

All that was left for me to do was to tell Siobhán. Telling her wasn't the same as telling my own flesh and blood. Neither Kate nor I could be sure how she would react. She had never made an issue of Kate and me living together, she had never alluded to it to either of us. I had no idea how her evangelical religion would inform her opinion on this matter.

When the moment was opportune, together in the kitchen, I told Siobhán the whole story.

'Does Mum know all this?'

'Every last word of it. She has known about John since he turned up the first time.'

'Well that's all that matters. It's not important what I think.'

'However I'd be interested to know what you think,' I said.

'Well for me it's a simple matter. If you loved each other as much as you say you did, that's fine. If it had been a one night stand and there was nothing between you that would be different. As the Bible tells us in so many ways, love is everything and I believe that what two people who love each other do to express their love is nobody else's business.'

What the Bible says was the last word for Siobhán and I wouldn't press her. I didn't point out to her that she was confusing two kinds of love, romantic love and love for humanity, as so many brides did when choosing readings for their weddings.

At this time Siobhán was three or four months into her nursing course. It was an opportune moment for me to ask her more about it.

'So far it's all academic, all theory. I won't have much to tell you until we start on the wards.' With Siobhán I had tried, not always successfully, to avoid the 'years ago' or 'when I was young' line. I believed that while there was much that was better about the old days, on balance modern times were preferable. Each generation carries within it the capacity to deal with its own issues, but if each new generation is wise it will take account of the wisdom of previous generations, often honed on bitter experience. Some parts of the Bible recount great wisdom based on the astute observation of the experience of a variety of people and communities. These parts of the Bible are valuable. Some parts of the Bible that purport to give accounts of the world and the universe from a pre-scientific age understandably can be seen from today's perspective to be fallacious. As for the bits that purport to know the mind of a creator God and his scheme of salvation, they're pure fantasy. They have been created by humans and the belief that they are infallibly true has been the cause of more pain and suffering in the world than we can fathom.

In essence the human condition is as it ever was. Each new generation works at its value system in the context of its humanity and its approach to living. Some people learn from the past and some people never learn. Where people don't learn it is usually ego, pride, power, all leading to delusion, mild or great, that get in the way. The aphorism tells us that history repeats itself. Why did Hitler not learn from Napoleon's experience of Russian winters? That is because human nature is the same today as it ever was. That is what the Church calls original sin, the only doctrine of the Church that still made any sense to me in that it is a credible account of our human nature. We never get over being born. What theologians call our 'fallen' nature developed as an integral part of the evolution of the species from the beginning and became evident from the struggle for survival. Our nature as human beings focuses all of us on trying to find some security in order to survive and function in this mysterious world. This causes people in a myriad of ways to behave at the expense of others to look for security in ego, status, money and power and of course religion. Religion based on belief in a transcendent God and his scheme of salvation claims to be the only way, but it causes the problem it purports to solve; throughout history religion has been the source of division, bitterness, hatred, wars and the most unfathomable evil that war brings. If we only had societies based on ethics, the moral code that has evolved with the species and is universally accepted we'd be better off. In one form or another, this moral code has been incorporated into the teaching of all the world's great wise men. It is not dependent upon the metaphysical assumptions of religious people and does not emanate from a transcendent God. It has been honed from human experience as the species evolved. Human beings did not have to wait for a God to tell them it was wrong to kill another member of their tribe, steal his possessions or make love to his woman. This code is observed, or at least subscribed to, equally by religious people, and by people who do not believe in God. If we were to pass it on to the next generation as the most important thing we can give them, instead of the metaphysical fairy tales of religion, the world would be a better place. The dissension, bitterness and hatred that have been generated by the defence of the metaphysical fantasies of religion have made for a great deal of the pain and suffering in the world. I believed that Siobhán's desire to nurse was a way to serve other people. How far it came from what she believed about God and salvation I didn't know and I had no wish to discuss with her. Life is an adventure in forgiveness. If mutual respect and acceptance of diversity were the norm it would make for peaceful contented communities. This, however, requires the maturity that accepts diversity amongst people; maturity that does not claim to have the one and only truth that must be imposed on other people. Imposing religious or theological conformity on others has been responsible for appalling bitterness, hatred and war throughout history just as much as war has been caused by the lust for power of emperors, kings and evil lunatics like Hitler, Stalin, Pol Pot and many more.

These were the issues that interested me, but I had no desire to upset or disturb the religious beliefs of anybody, no matter how false I believed their beliefs to be, unless they wanted to talk about them. I certainly did not want to upset Siobhán, who after difficult early teenage years had recently, through a particular kind of religion, become a happier person.

Both Kate and I in our early days had known girls that had trained as nurses. In those days nursing had been an exclusively female preserve. There were men in Siobhán's class. In those days too at least ninety per cent of doctors were male. By this time less than fifty per cent of newly qualified doctors were men. In most of its facets the world of medicine had changed, not just medically and scientifically, but in personnel.

When, in contrast to the days of Kate's and my childhood, a matter of the modern world arose in conversation with Siobhán, she would mock me in a sing-song voice: '*When I was a child telephones had handles. You wound them up, got on to the postmistress who put you through to your number and listened to the conversation. She was the best informed person in the district.*' Siobhán was disappointed if I didn't accompany her word for word and add: '*and sometimes without even trying the number she would say: "they're in Dublin for the day and won't be back till evening.*" She would also say to me from time to time things like:

'Will you tell Mum to stop worrying, I can look after myself. I know more about the world out there than she does.'

Kate was secretly pleased that Siobhán and Judy would be going to separate colleges, since for some time she had been anxious that they were spending so much time exclusively together. Kate and I were fond of Judy and knew they would still be best friends, but this would mean they would both have the opportunity to make new friends too.

'You know,' I broached, 'that nurses these days are superior beings compared with nurses years ago. They don't have to empty bedpans, clean patients' false teeth and perform all the menial tasks that they once did and at the other end I believe they do things these days that were once done only by doctors.'

'Yes, I know,' she said with a mock weary tone. 'We went over all that in early lectures. Things have moved on since Florence Nightingale you know.'

'Who, by the way,' I said, 'was what the lads at work would call a "walkin' divil."'

'That's not fair. She was a tough cookie, but you had to be tough as a woman in those days to get things done. All she did came from her religion and she was quite a mystic.'

'I'm nervous of mystics,' I said, and Siobhán without a word began to play an imaginary violin.

'When you're my age, you'll repeat yourself too,' I said.

'I bet I won't. Having lived with two wrinklies for so long I've learned the lesson. I'll never repeat myself to anyone.'

'What about the men in your class. How do you get on with them?'

'They're all right, but they'll get most of the top jobs.'

'That's because women take time out to have babies,' I said.

'Not all women have babies. What about matrons in the past when hospitals ran on oiled wheels and there was no such thing as the hospital bug?'

'Until recently male nurses were as rare as hens' teeth,' I said, 'there weren't any.' Siobhán didn't respond. 'How does Judy like medical school?' I asked.

'She loves it. It's what she always wanted to do. She'll make a great doctor. There's nothing men can do that women can't do better.'

I took up my imaginary violin and played a few bars. 'What was it you said about never repeating yourself?' She grinned and started to clear the table.

CHAPTER 8

Kate's immense relief that Siobhán was now at university and on an even keel was dented by a development at work. A new school principal started with the school year. All her staff had been sorry to see Nan, as she was known affectionately to them, retire. She had been a good administrator and a kindly motherly figure to her teachers and pupils alike. She was, however, no pushover when it came to difficulties with teachers, parents or pupils, but she always seemed to have been able to negotiate in such a way that rarely left anybody feeling hard done by. Kate kept me posted on developments blow by blow.

The new principal was a younger man. It wasn't long before it became clear to the staff that as well as gender he was a different proposition entirely from his predecessor. This was his first appointment as principal and the staff was encouraged when he sent a circular to them saying some predictable things ending with: 'I look forward to getting to know you and working with you in the interests of the pupils.'

'He sounds OK,' one of the younger teachers offered in the staffroom at the first coffee break after they had received the circular. A senior member of staff opined that to her the whole tenor of the circular was that now that he had arrived the project of educating the children would begin in earnest. It didn't say so in so many words but it was clear from a careful reading between the lines that the new principal was saying that education in this school up to now had been deficient, but from now on under his control it would become the genuine article.

In the first couple of weeks of term the principal organised a schedule of individual interviews with teachers. These were arranged in order of seniority. The first was with the long-serving vice-principal who had applied for the job and hadn't been appointed. This was a difficult interview for her which she recounted to the others in detail. He had patronised her and made it clear that he was in charge. She described him as one of those people who in discussion of a topic will engage in an exchange of a few sentences then suddenly draw the conversation to a close with a final and definitive statement designed to be the last word on the matter, and indicating not only that the discussion is at an end, but that it has been concluded in clear support of his point of view. When he had decided that the interview with the vice-principal was over he said he hoped he would have her loyalty. She told him that she would do as she had always done, which was to work to the best of her ability in the interests of the pupils and of the school.

Kate recounted to me in detail her own interview with him:

'I gather that you haven't been teaching here for very long,' the principal started.

'Relatively, no. I have done most of my teaching in the country.'

'Country children are different from city children,' he said.

'Country children are savvier these days than they used to be,' Kate replied, 'I haven't found much difference really. Have you taught in a rural school?'

'No, but my family came originally from the country.'

'You have a daughter.' He had done his homework, where, or with whom Kate didn't know.

'Yes, she has just started at university.'

'What's she studying?'

'Nursing.'

'You're married of course?' he said. Kate bridled. She didn't like where the interview was going. She had expected it to be about her teaching; new methods, subjects, the age group she preferred to teach, extra-curricular work and so on. Unlike her, she immediately took a firm line.

'You're not allowed to ask me that.'

'Yes I am. This is not an interview for employment.'

'My work as a teacher is a legitimate concern of yours, but my private life is not.'

'As you are well aware this is a Catholic school in which a Catholic ethos must be maintained.'

'I'm Catholic, and yes, I am married.'

'And you live with your husband?'

'Who I live with is entirely my own affair. I'm perfectly happy to discuss with you my professional role in the school, but not my private life.'

'But it is a well established principle that the private lives of teachers must be in accord with the ethos of the school. I can see that you are upset. Will we leave it at that and we'll talk again in a week or so?'

Kate did not reply, stood up and left. She went immediately to the vice-principal and recounted the interview to her. The vice-principal was furious:

'There's a fifth columnist in the ranks. It could be a teacher or a parent or someone on the board. We'll talk about this later. In the meantime don't worry; those days have gone.'

Kate was in a state when she arrived home and told me the story.

'Contact your union,' I advised her, 'they'll know what he can and cannot ask.'

Kate was a fully paid-up member. Some of Kate's colleagues had allowed their union membership to lapse but all of them had re-joined within weeks of the arrival of the new principal.

'He can't ask you questions about your private life,' the union official said. 'He's trying to turn back the clock. If he persists let me know and I'll be in touch with him.'

Kate was badly thrown by the attitude of the new principal to her. She had had an excellent relationship with Nan who was well aware of her domestic arrangements. She loved her job and knew that, even if the new principal were prevented from making an issue of Kate and I not being married he could make life difficult for her. She became preoccupied with the matter and, unlike her, she began to lose sleep. She would lie awake for hours going over and over the whole thing in her mind, and of course at night it was a hundred times worse than it really was. Her appetite was affected and I found it impossible to raise a smile on any topic.

Her anxiety was alleviated somewhat by the knowledge that she wasn't alone. He was picking up on things and niggling with other teachers too, but with none of them was it such a central issue as with her. It became clear that the new principal wouldn't be working *with* his staff, but *over* them. Teachers were complaining to the vice-principal, who was representing their complaints, as diplomatically as she was able, to the principal, but she made no headway with him. The school secretary didn't hide the fact that she could not abide him, and hinted that if he didn't change his attitude she'd find herself another job.

There were a couple of teachers who were less critical of the new principal than the others. They didn't come out openly and say they supported him in his attitude to school ethos, but they certainly had some regard for his views. The trouble with staffroom conversation is that it seldom lasts longer than the extent of a coffee break and even then like-minded tend to consort with like-minded so that a spectrum of views is seldom aired. Conversation in Kate's staffroom in those days was seldom other than about the new regime. It was clear that some believed that criticism of, and disregard for, religion had gone too far. There was obviously universal acceptance that child abuse had damaged the credibility of the Church, and that the Church's cover-up to protect its reputation at the expense of children was even worse, but there was a danger of throwing out the baby with the bathwater. Few would have disagreed with this in principle, but most did not see that the answer was to turn back the clock to the old days of child indoctrination: 'We know the truth and if you want to save your soul believe what we tell you, and don't forget everybody who disagrees with us is wrong. If you believe what we tell you, you will get to heaven, and if you don't, you'll go to hell. As the Pope had said recently: "Hell hasn't gone away.'"

Kate was brought up with this attitude but the world had changed. Even the official Church had changed its attitude from those days. The obsession used to be about saving souls; getting people into heaven. The emphasis, without losing sight of salvation, nowadays had changed to how people behaved in order to make for a caring loving Christian community here on earth. It was about helping to relieve pain and suffering amongst people. Despite all of this the Church's obsession with sex had not gone away. That Kate and I had not been through a marriage ceremony did not affect one whit the quality of her teaching children. I have no doubt that even if we had had a civil marriage it would not have been acceptable to the new principal. Not all of the mindless superstition of the past had gone away. There was still the odd teacher around who on the weekend of an All-Ireland final would pray in class that the county's team would win. Would the new principal reprimand such a teacher for imposing such patent nonsense on innocent and suggestible minds?

There was incredulity amongst most of the staff about the attitude of the new regime. Some of those that were most outraged talked of a lightning strike. Most were in favour of leaving it to the teachers' union, and that was what they did.

The vice-principal spoke to the union. The conversation centred largely on the fact that Kate was not married to the man she was living with. It was a surprise that his informant did not also tell the principal that the man she was living with was a lapsed Protestant cleric, or maybe they did. The principal was censorious of other members of staff too. In one case he pointed out to a younger teacher that she was not appropriately dressed to teach young children – sex again. The vice-principal left the union in no doubt where almost all of the staff stood on the matters they brought up. The official in turn left the teachers in no doubt where the union stood on all these matters; on the side of the teachers. The principal had not spoken to Kate again about her marital status. She loved her job, she loved the children, but the whole affair unsettled her seriously and made difficult any dealings she had with the principal.

The principal's attitude to almost everything made for problems amongst staff that they consciously tried not to allow to affect their teaching. Parents came to teachers to complain about things that were outside their control and some of them approached the principal but found him entirely unapproachable and sometimes downright rude. The issue was raised at every meeting of the board of management, so that the parish priest, who was chairman, was in no doubt where things stood. The principal was in control but so removed was he that he wasn't even aware that his staff were in revolt.

The union arranged a meeting between the principal, the vice-principal and a union official. Beforehand they spoke to Kate and asked for her permission to recount her conversation with the principal about her marital status. Kate agreed but this increased her anxiety and she felt the onus of responsibility for what had now become a serious matter. Her contretemps with the principal was the centrepiece, though by no means the only contentious issue to be levelled against him. She was fearful that whatever the outcome it would make her life at school impossible.

The day following the meeting the vice-principal held a meeting for the union official to meet all members of teaching staff. The official laid out the union position on the private lives of teachers and then recounted the substance of the meeting they had had with the principal. It was clear that the principal would not be happy but he would have no option but to accept it. He brought the matter to the management committee, but despite the fact that the parish priest was chairman, the committee passed a resolution to abide by the position of the union.

The principal's attitude became sullen and he would barely respond to Kate when school business made it necessary for her to talk to him. His attitude to the rest of the staff became easier but he kept his distance unless it was necessary for them to consult him. According to the vice-principal he was in a permanent sulk because he did not have the support of the management committee. Despite reassurances to the contrary Kate felt responsible for what had happened, but by the end of the Easter term things appeared to have settled down.

On the first day of the summer term, to the surprise and delight of staff, the management committee posted a notice on the staffroom notice-board to say that the principal had tendered his resignation and would be leaving at the end of the school year.

Around this time another event unsettled Kate. One Saturday morning at breakfast Siobhán announced:

'Judy and I are planning to move into a flat together.' Kate did not reply, so although it was the kind of personal matter for Siobhán on which I would not normally comment, I filled the awkward silence:

'How'll you manage? You'll miss my cooking.'

'I know, but before I leave you can teach me how to boil eggs as well as you do.'

'Can you afford it?' Kate asked.

'That's why I'm bringing it up now; I'll need help with the rent.'

'It's not just rent. It's food, electricity and lots of other bits and pieces,' said Kate.

'I know, but we're not moving until September and I'll have an allowance from the hospital then. I'll just need a top up for my half of the rent. If we still lived in the country you'd have to pay rent for me, so it's no different.'

'Yes, but we don't live in the country,' said Kate. As usual I stayed out of it, and again neither of them asked my opinion or called on me to support their case.

Since coming to the city Judy had been Siobhán's only real friend. She had been a good influence on her at a time when having left her friends behind, she was unsettled and unhappy. Judy was a city girl and Siobhán had learned a great deal from her that stood to her in negotiating the difficult transition from country to city. Kate was delighted with their friendship but came to be unsure that its exclusiveness was wise.

'There's plenty of time,' Kate said to me when Siobhán had left the kitchen, 'I'll let it sit until she brings it up again.'

During the controversy about the principal, Kate had given serious consideration to resigning from her job and finding another. She didn't relish the idea of starting afresh in a new school as she was aware that all schools were coping with some issue or other. She received the news of the principal's resignation with great relief. She was even more relieved when during the summer she had word that Marie, the vice-principal had been appointed to replace him. Marie had worked closely with Nan and would be the same kind of principal that Nan had been.

'Why did they not appoint Marie in the first place?' Kate had wondered.

'Don't you know that a man will always do the same job better than a woman?' I replied.

'Oh God,' Kate said, 'will they never learn.'

Kate now looked forward to the new term in the autumn. But she wasn't sure about Siobhán moving into a flat with Judy:

'Don't worry,' I offered, 'they'll both be making new friends in their respective colleges, and when Siobhán is on the wards a whole new world will open up for her. Anyway they are both adult now and they are entitled to make their own decisions.'

Kate remained silent.

I went on: 'Topics from the Bible don't arise for discussion with Siobhán as often as they used to, but as long as they go to their Sunday morning meeting they are unlikely to go off the rails.'

Siobhán and Judy passed their first year exams. They had some time off and then both had hospital placements until their academic year started in the autumn. In the end Kate agreed to fund Siobhán to share a flat with Judy and they moved in together at the beginning of September. It was more of an adjustment for Kate and me than either of us anticipated. I missed Siobhán, but Kate missed her terribly. It changed the way Kate and I related at home, not in any adverse way; it was just different. Siobhán kept in touch by phone and on her first visit home she gave us an account of how well she and Judy were getting on.

'Waking in the morning, getting up in time to have some breakfast is the biggest problem. Coming back in the evening and chatting about our day while we get dinner is great.'

'Which of you is the cook?' I asked, 'and I hope you don't over do the boiled eggs.'

'Judy doesn't like soft boiled eggs. We share the cooking. We share everything, and we're very happy.'

Kate was relieved that it was all working well for Siobhán and Judy and she and I soon adjusted to being alone together. I felt that Kate had coped with a lot recently and needed a good break, so towards the end of the summer we went on an expensive holiday to Florence where Kate could pursue the one great interest that could take her mind off her worries, Renaissance Art.

It worked. Kate came home the better for her holiday, and of course I enjoyed it immensely, not least because it meant so much to Kate. Whatever chance she had of sharing her great enthusiasm with some of her colleagues at work, the chances of me having a response from the lads in the warehouse to my holiday were pretty remote.

CHAPTER 9

I was back to work on the Monday after we arrived home from Italy. At the tea break mid-morning the joker of the warehouse asked:

'Where did you go on your holidays?'

'Italy.'

'Did you go and see the Pope?'

'What do you think?'

'You hardly did, I suppose? Is there an atheist Pope?'

'Believe it or not there were a few popes over the centuries that the scholars tell us were atheist, but if you're asking about today, I suppose Richard Dawkins might qualify.'

'That fella' gives me a pain in the arse,' one of the others said. 'He has all the answers.'

'I don't much like him myself, but I can't disagree with a word he says.'

'Well if you didn't go to see the Pope where did you go?'

'Florence.'

'They're at the bottom of the Italian first division.'

'And that's where they'll stay,' one of the others came in and the conversation went off on football for the rest of the break.

Kate had another week before she went back to school. Until now she had not been able to contact Marie to congratulate her on her appointment. She phoned her to say how delighted she was and to wish her well.

'It would have saved us all a lot of trouble and stress if you'd been appointed in the first place.'

Marie made it plain that not everyone would agree, but she knew that most did. She was well aware that the few that thought 'your man' was on the right lines largely kept their counsel. She was most grateful for Kate's support. Between parents, children and teachers a school principal can't win.

'You took the brunt of it,' Marie said. 'I hope you had a good summer.'

'We're not long back from a wonderful holiday in Italy, and I'm ready for a new start.'

When school began there was a changed atmosphere. It was back to Nan's day when everyone took it for granted that the task was to work for the children. There was a return to co-operation between parents and teachers. Teachers could go into the office without getting an earful about 'your man' from the secretary. There were of course one or two teachers and the odd parent that were never satisfied and always had a gripe to make, but that wasn't new. It's all part of the diversity of people in the real world and we have to learn to live with it.

Siobhán was spending time in hospital working on the wards and loving it. She didn't mind the long hours on her feet as long as she was working with patients. She was well able to cope with the academic and this was what she had always wanted to do. She and Judy dropped in occasionally and often came for Sunday lunch.

That autumn life settled into a routine. I looked forward to retirement and Kate was back to teaching again.

One Monday morning I had a phone call in work to say that Kate had collapsed at school and had been taken to hospital. I went immediately. I found her in A&E with a team of doctors and nurses attending to her. I had to wait for what seemed like an age before I was allowed to see her. Finally a young doctor came to speak to me.

'She's stable at the moment, but we won't know for certain until we have the result of blood tests if she has had a heart attack. In the meantime we have taken all the precautions we can. You can see her for a minute now before we move her to the cardiac unit.'

I pulled back the curtain of the cubicle. There was a nurse with her monitoring a machine to which Kate was attached. She was lying with her eyes closed and didn't hear me coming. The nurse looked up and acknowledged my presence. I stood for a few seconds looking at those gentle features that for me had always reflected the beautiful person that lay behind them. I took her hand. She opened her eyes and a gentle smile caused a surge of emotion to bring tears to my eyes. She was clearly heavily sedated and I had to strain to hear what she said:

'I love you.' Tears rolled down my cheeks as I leaned forward and kissed her gently on the forehead.

'I love you too,' I said, and in that moment I was aware of just how much.

'It's going to be all right,' Kate said slowly and quietly and closed her eyes again. I stood and watched and was aware that as long as we had each other nothing else mattered. The curtains were pulled back by a porter who had come to take Kate to the coronary care unit. As he moved the bed, with the nurse beside it wheeling the machine, she didn't waken. I released her hand and went back to find the doctor.

'If you wait for twenty minutes or so until they settle her you can go up and see her again.'

I went outside for air and had exactly the same experience I remembered when Jennifer had been in intensive care: the world outside was going about its business oblivious of the fear, the hope, the confusion of emotions that were flooding my whole being and making it impossible for me to think clearly.

I didn't know whether to phone Siobhán then or wait until the results of the blood tests were back in the hope that I might be able to tell her it wasn't a heart attack. I was glad that Kate had not been brought to the hospital where Siobhán was doing her placement. I decided to phone her and I told her as much as I knew.

'I'm off duty in half an hour and I'll come then.'

By the time Siobhán arrived the doctors had established that Kate had had a heart attack. Siobhán went in to see her mother and then we left together with the assurance from the doctor that we could see her again, one at a time, in the evening.

'There's a history of heart in her family,' Siobhán said.

Kate's heart attack was mild; little more than a warning. She was home in a week and Marie had arranged for a teaching substitute for her. Her medical certificate was open ended in order to see how quickly she recovered.

I was amazed how I remembered some of the parallels with Jennifer. I remembered how I had been called to the hospital, Jennifer too had been in intensive care attached to a machine monitored by a nurse. For both I went over in my mind the thoughts of being left alone. When Jennifer died I had no idea that Kate and I would become lovers. If Kate died there was no chance that at this stage of my life I would get together with anybody else. I had loved Jennifer, but she had abandoned me in pursuit of her love affair with alcohol long before she died. I could remember her only with my head. I recalled her sharp intelligence; sharper than mine. I remembered the immense respect I had had for her capacity to be her own person and yet in the early years of our marriage, despite the fact that it really wasn't her scene, she supported me by being the best she was able to be as a dutiful rector's wife. These memories were cerebral. They touched nothing in my heart.

Now my heart was full of love and hope for Kate. I had occasional bouts of foreboding, but dispelled them by reminding myself of the positive prognosis the doctor had given. With medication, exercise and a sensible diet Kate would lead a normal life again. It was no trouble to her to take the pills, but she loved her grub and neither of us took enough exercise. There would have to be changes.

Kate went back to work for a few weeks before Christmas. Each day when she arrived home from school she went for a rest and in the New Year she was more or less back to normal, but her resolution about diet and exercise gradually faded.

In June, towards the end of the academic year, Kate had a phone call from Siobhán to make an appointment to come home to meet us together. This was unusual; she dropped in casually from time to time and mostly we were both in. There was little that Siobhán talked to her mother about that she didn't include me. We had two days to wait in which the imagination of us both ran riot. We covered every conceivable possibility. On the evening, before she arrived, Kate and I moved into the sitting-room and waited. Siobhán arrived; she still had her own key.

'We're in here,' Kate called. Siobhán came in and as always she kissed us both. She sat down and we made small talk until it became too much for Kate.

'You wanted to see us,' she said.

'I did. I have something to tell you.' She paused. 'Judy and I are splitting up.' It was the one thing Kate and I had not speculated. We never dreamed of it. 'Judy has fallen in love with a woman in her class in college, and yes, in case you were in any doubt, we were partners, lovers or whatever you called it in your day – if you even knew about it.'

I waited for Kate to speak and she didn't. She looked shocked and I didn't know if it was because of the confirmation of the nature of Judy and Siobhán's relationship or because it had broken up.

'I'm very sorry,' I said.

'So am I,' Siobhán said with a voice that broke on those three short words, and then she dissolved into a flood of tears. Kate went to her, put her arm around her and hugged her. It took Siobhán the best part of five minutes before she spoke again:

'I had no idea,' Siobhán said. 'When Judy told me I thought she was joking. I couldn't take it in. I thought we were together for life. I'm still in love with her, but she has fallen out of love with me.' Siobhán broke down again.

My immediate thought was that her father had deserted her and now the one person who had brought stability and purpose to her life when it was in turmoil, and with whom she would spend the rest of her life, had deserted her too.

Siobhán sat close to her mother who stroked her hair. Eventually Kate spoke:

'I know, my precious daughter, this will be of no comfort to you now, but things are often for the best. When your father left me my life was in pieces. Only for you I would have found it hard to keep going and look what happened – slowly, with John and you a wonderful new life evolved. I know what you're going through; I went through it and I promise you I will never say this to you again. In the meantime I will do everything I can to support you, and I know that John will too and through these dark days we'll both be here for you as a new day dawns and you are yourself again.'

Siobhán lifted her head, looked her mother straight in the eye and said:

'That's very poetical, Mum. Where did that come from? Wherever it came from, thank you.' She sat up, reached across, put her hand on my knee and said:

'Thank you, John.'

'Your bedroom is here,' Kate said, 'we haven't taken in a lodger.'

'And if you do decide to come back,' I added, 'you can have that perfectly boiled egg for breakfast again.' Siobhán smiled faintly.

'Judy says she can't account for how all this happened. It just did. We still have a lot to sort out.' We talked on for a while, until Siobhán suddenly stood up:

'I'll be in touch.' She kissed us both and left.

We both knew in our different ways something of what Siobhán was going through. We had both known what it was to put painful memories of the past behind us in order to survive and to give some new shape to our lives.

We had talked before about Siobhán and Judy's relationship and we suspected the way it was. That wasn't a problem for Kate and it certainly wasn't a problem for me. Siobhán was the dependent one. If nothing else Judy had brought Siobhán safely through a turbulent period in her short life, and for that alone Kate was grateful.

I had always thought of 'falling in love' as the first in a series of devices of nature designed to ensure the survival of the species. If there was no falling in love and if nature hadn't designed sex to be intensely pleasurable, people mightn't bother and humanity might die out. This of course wouldn't apply in the case of Judy and Siobhán, but then nature isn't always consistent. Some of its achievements are a bit hit and miss – Friday evening and Monday morning people, and it is nobody's business to blame the people themselves for the carelessness of their producer. If we are half normal at all, and few of us are, in fact are there any, it is up to us to support those whom nature has set off in life with all kinds of disadvantage. It's hard to escape the conclusion that humans are little more than the playthings of nature. Nature in some of its aspects is wonderful, magical and miraculous and in others it is unfathomably cruel and uncaring.

This business of falling in love is at the core of human existence. After birth, falling in love and dying are the two most important parts of human experience. They have the greatest consequence: falling in love has most consequence for ourselves and dying has most consequence for others. Imagine what life would be like if there were no falling in love and if we lived for ever. No romantic art, novels or films, no undertakers, graveyards or ghosts and above all no religion as we know it, no waiting for a second coming. Eternal life would be here on earth. Married to the same person for a thousand years or more. All unthinkable. We're much better off with the system we have, bad and all as it is, and of which it is difficult to make sense. We are better to fall in love, procreate and die than to live for ever, here or elsewhere. Nature has devised a good system and it works.

The older I became the less I knew about anything, and the less sense I could make of what humans do to each other; man's inhumanity to man. We don't choose to come here; that results from people falling in love, or at least having sex, over which we have no control. I don't think we choose who to fall in love with. We don't choose the 'when' and the 'how' of our dying. While we are alive there is no shortage of people who claim the right to tell us how to live. How should we live? 'Should' implies that there is someone somewhere who knows or has laid down the way. Sometimes I think that the lads in the yard have a better handle on it all than I have. They are not cursed with the facility to analyse constantly what it is all about. They get on with life, follow football, back the odd horse, drink a few pints and harm nobody. In a crisis of their own or that of a neighbour, they behave with decency and compassion. They know innately that not everybody starts with the same chance in life. Some people are dealt a wonderful hand and make an utter hames of it and some are dealt a rotten hand and are heroic in how they play it. They are not hung up on the findings of research or the result of opinion polls. The only serious delusion under which they suffer, apart from believing there is a God, is that if they won the lottery it would solve all their problems.

Perhaps these work colleagues of mine envy Derek, the boss, with his top of the range Volvo and all the accoutrements of success, but when they heard he was having an affair with his secretary they felt sorry for his wife. Human decency. Those are two of the main things that mark people off from each other – money and human decency. Most have one or the other, quite a few have neither and some, but very few, have both.

Siobhán left that evening to go back to Judy to cope with rejection. No matter how gentle, no matter how being usurped in Judy's affections by another, somebody she didn't even know, and innocent though she was, as far as we knew, in the whole affair, it wasn't her fault that she was the one in pain. Judy was the one living with the excitement of a new love but suffering the problem of discarding the old one wanting to cause, we assumed, as little pain as possible to Siobhán. How did this all come about? How had Judy's love for Siobhán run its course for her but not for Siobhán? Had Judy's new love been active or passive in attracting Judy's affection? Was Judy active or passive? Was there any way in which Siobhán was to blame? In human conflict there are usually faults on both sides. How could we, a third party, without knowing the intimacies of what passes between two people, have any hope of making a fair judgment? Then it is not the place of a third party, unless asked, to make any judgment. Unless they ask for help, people just have to sort things out for themselves. Knowing right from wrong and acting accordingly is wonderful in principle, but in affairs of the heart it is another matter, or is it? Violating the principle is what causes the trouble. Neither Kate nor I did, or could have, come together while Jennifer was alive. That we might have done did not occur to either of us. At least that was how it was for me. Nobody knows all the thoughts of another no matter how close they are. There is a part of all of us that we do not reveal, an inner kernel of the self that the self does not allow to be subject to the scrutiny of any other person no matter how much love and trust there is. If there is too much of this inner kernel, it can lead to profound loneliness. Siobhán was young to suffer this loss. The most that Kate and I could do was to be there for her. Before she went that night we left her in no doubt that we would support her no matter what, and her home was still here for her. The famous quotation from Robert Frost came to mind; '*Home is the place where, when you have to go there/They have to take you in.'/ 'I should have called it/Something you somehow haven't to deserve.*' With Siobhán, however, it wasn't a case of 'have to'. We were glad to be the home she would come to, and no, she didn't have to deserve it.

Siobhán moved back the following week. Kate and I were careful not to ask her any questions; simply to listen to what she chose to tell us. Her first morning home was a Saturday. Siobhán arrived down to breakfast in her dressing-gown. It was clear that she wanted to talk.

'I can't understand how I didn't see it coming. Judy told me that her love for me had been wearing thin for months, and even looking back I didn't see any signs.'

'Loving somebody isn't an exact science,' I said. 'It's a whole complex of emotions, or perhaps it is truths, that we are loyal to as best we can. It involves the acceptance of faults and imperfections in the other but loving them all the same and the better two people can do that the better their lives together will be. The crucial issue is that we are all human and from time to time we all fail. When that happens the only way forward is for contrition and forgiveness.'

'That's the only sermon I ever heard you preach,' Siobhán said.

'And the only one I've ever heard him preach either,' Kate added.

'And it's the last one you'll ever hear, even though I don't consider it was a sermon at all,' I said, 'just a few thoughts.'

Kate and I were acutely aware of the sheer hopelessness of being able to do or say anything to alleviate the emotional pain of another. We learned that words were pretty useless and that a smile, a gentle touch, a gesture, a thoughtful action had some chance of communicating the understanding and unconditional support we wanted to convey. There is little that can be done to help somebody to alleviate the pain of unrequited love. The little that can be done is simply to survive, to endure, to wait until the reality of the old aphorism, 'time is a great healer', becomes apparent.

Slowly over the weeks and months the devastation that Siobhán had experienced began to heal. A new normality descended upon the routine of the house. Kate went to school, Siobhán went to college or hospital and I went to work.

Kate and I re-established a walking habit of sorts including our Sunday morning walk along the beach followed by Sunday newspapers, but I was finding I could walk less and less. After a few months Siobhán had learned to smile again, just a little, and we looked forward in time to hearing her laugh. She went out occasionally with a group of friends from college. Slowly we became aware that she went to things with a girlfriend, but she didn't talk much about that. What she did say was intended to convey clearly to us that this friendship was platonic.

In less than two years I would retire. A prospect to which I looked forward since my work at the warehouse was tedious. I wouldn't miss the work, but I would miss the lads. I had worked in a bank; it was a desert. It gave me a monthly wage, but it was a wasted time in my life. When I became a full-time student I came alive. From there I went to working with people in parishes to be with people in their joys and in their sorrows; to celebrate with them and to support them in their troubles of one kind or another. I was the leader in creating and supporting community and providing ritual to enable people to express some kind of a response to the mystery of being human. Some thought there was no mystery at all. It was about believing what they were taught as children; that there was a God in heaven that watched them as they lived out their lives and after death if they had behaved well they would go one way and if they had behaved badly they would go the other. They left the details to the Church and trusted the clergy to know it all. Largely speaking, the clergy didn't disturb their childish faith or the stories and the simplistic system that purported to make sense of the whole thing. Clergy were not prepared to tell lay people that the stories were composed by humans to convey truths as they saw them. People took these stories literally for the best part of two thousand years when for many people the stories had outlived their credibility and the usefulness for which they had been told in the first place. How many clergy, for example, at Christmas were prepared to tell their parishioners what scholarship over the years had made clear: historically there were no shepherds, there was no choir of angels, no stable, no wise men, but that this beautiful story was designed to convey what pre-scientific tribal scribes believed retrospectively about who Jesus was? The world has moved on since then and most of the doctrine to which the Church subscribes stretches the credulity of thoughtful people. For me my time in parishes was both satisfying and frustrating but the whole edifice of essential Church doctrine and teaching became incredible to me and made it impossible for me to stay. This was the right decision for me, as was my decision to enter the ministry in the first place. I had no regrets about either; both were right in their time.

I had learned that there were all sorts of people in the ordained ministry from people who were little more than adequately literate, to people who were highly qualified academically and who could have been successful academics. Some would hardly have survived if they had had to earn a living, and some would have been successful in whatever they turned their hand to in the real world. Clergy are paid a stipend to free them from having to earn a living in order to allow them to perform their clerical duties. Some of both kinds were good pastorally and some were hopeless with people. Some were good liturgically and conducted services of worship with great sensitivity. Some took services as if they were running the local mart and they moved around the church as if they were crossing a ploughed field. There were those who were determined to be clergy since they were children and those who came to it late. There were a lot of clergy sons in the ministry. Most, of any clerical hue, were interested in status and preferment; to become canons, deans, archdeacons and bishops. There were a few who had no interest in this kind of thing but just wanted to do the job well according to what they believed, whatever that was. I had little inkling of what any of them actually believed. Clergy didn't talk together about belief. I suspected, however, that most didn't believe as much as lay people thought they did. All human life is present amongst the clergy as it is amongst any group of people who do the same job. Clergy are afforded a status beyond what they deserve because they are considered to have a vocation that puts them in touch in a special way with the eternal in order to communicate and interpret it for the temporal.

I had had many colleagues that I respected and still do, and there were others whom I have no idea what they thought they were doing. The ministry of the Church is a fascinating patchwork of human abilities and motivations. Clergy through their work fill their personal needs. In the process they can do a great deal of good. Most Church members, clerical and lay, become absorbed in the institution and what it stands for, and because they have been indoctrinated in it they are unable to see how incredible its doctrine is in this day and age.

These reflections were stimulated by my thoughts on my retirement from my job as 'inspector of containers'. I often mused on whether it was a job with more or less status than Percy French's job as 'inspector of drains'. It wasn't creative or terribly fulfilling, but it helped me with the practicality of making my contribution to the household economy.

CHAPTER 10

Kate was happy with the new regime at school, however she didn't talk with the same enthusiasm about school as she had always done. She didn't recount the surprising and amusing things that children said and did and she demurred from extra-curricular activities. I couldn't work out if she had never regained her confidence since the confrontation and controversy during the reign of the religious whizz kid, or whether her illness had knocked the stuffing out of her physically or mentally or both. When I broached the subject she brushed me off with something like:

'I'm fine. Anno Domini; there's none of us getting younger.'

Siobhán did eventually laugh again; she was back to her old self as far as we could see, but there were the occasional moments of silent preoccupation that suggested to Kate and to me that her hurt had not entirely healed. She was absorbed in, and seemed to have had great satisfaction from, her study and her work. Just like Kate she had stopped talking about her work, but slowly this came back. She began to go out to social events with her class and even recounted to us something of how she had enjoyed them.

Little had changed at my work. One day when my retirement date was approaching, at our lunch-time sandwiches one of the lads asked me:

'Will you miss us?'

'Of course I'll miss you, but I have to be honest; I'll get over it.'

'And what'll you do?'

'I won't need to get up so early, and I'll have plenty of time to read.'

'What'll you read? Books?'

'Yes, books.'

'Books about what? Maeve Binchy books? I do see women readin' them on the train comin' in to work.'

'No, not Maeve Binchy. History.'

'Jesus, history; I hated that at school. You want to keep pigeons. If you get someone to build a loft, I'll stock it for you.'

'That's good of you, but as you know I know nothing about pigeons except that they always find their way home and as I've told you before when you race them you should 'free' them or 'let them out' this 'liberate' business is just trying to be posh.'

'In the war they used them to send messages.'

'Yes, I know that, but I'd prefer a good book.'

'Well, if you change your mind I'll stock a loft for you.'

They made me promise that on the evening of my last day at work I'd be sure to go to the pub with them. Any time I went with them after work they knew I would have only one drink. I agreed to go and as it was a special occasion I promised I'd have two drinks.

'Jayze, you'd want to mind you don't lose the run o' yourself.'

When the others were onto their third pint I decided it was time for me to leave.

'Colm wants to say somethin'.' Colm stood up:

'John, you were a great fella' to work with and we'll miss you and we bought you this.' He handed me a parcel that was obviously a book. I opened it: 'The History of Ireland Since the Famine'. For a few seconds I couldn't speak to thank them. I collected myself and did; in a few sentences I told them what working with them meant to me and one of them said:

'And if we win the lotto we'll give you a shout.'

It didn't take me long to adjust to retirement. Arthritis was developing quickly in my back and my legs and I couldn't have gone on working much longer. It was only a short time before I had to concede that for other than around the house, where I used the furniture, I had to use a stick. My plan for when I retired was to get up early and make breakfast for Kate and Siobhán. This was not possible. Were I to do that, I would first have needed Kate to help me out of bed and down the stairs which would have defeated the purpose. I stayed on in bed until they had both gone to work and then I had all the time in the world to manoeuvre myself downstairs. Even stooping to stack the lower shelf of the dishwasher gave me gyp. I had to put the dishes beside it and sit on a chair. I couldn't walk far and began to put on weight.

One morning, about a year after I retired, I dozed on after I had heard Kate's alarm clock go off. When I woke, her bedside light wasn't lit. She was still asleep. She would be late for work. I turned on my own light and shook her, she didn't move. I felt her forehead. She was cold. I shouted for Siobhán. She couldn't find a pulse.

Needless to say, I knew that either of us could have died first, but I never countenanced the possibility that it might be Kate, even after her heart warning. I was older than she was: on average men don't live as long as women and both her parents lived to greater ages than my parents did, but we can't presume on nature.

Kate had left no instructions. I wanted Siobhán to make decisions about her funeral, and she was clear in her mind that the burial should take place in Kate's home place in Cork. Arranging funerals, as I had learned during my time in parishes, can be a tricky business. Families are funny and are often not at one in what they think is the right thing to do. Siobhán left the details to me and I dealt with Kate's brother, Eamon, with whom I could work well.

'I'll look after things at this end,' he said, 'Una might be tricky, but don't worry I'll handle her.'

Una was the one that Kate referred to as 'my religious sister'. She was married to a farmer who had two brothers priests and a sister a nun. Eamon had once told me that by all accounts 'the nun', as he always referred to her, was a hard ticket who believed that being religious didn't require a person to be miserable and to deny their humanity. Eamon had once heard the nun say that her older priest brother, who was the patriarch of their family, had been corrupted by piety and then added as though it was the most natural thing in the world to say about one's big brother, priest or no priest, that he was 'a pain in the arse'.

I arranged for the undertaker the family always used to come for Kate from West Cork. The finality of her death only struck me outside the funeral home as the undertaker closed the back door of the hearse on the coffin. People had shaken hands and offered sympathy to Siobhán and me. Family friends and Kate's work colleagues stood around waiting. I stood with Mary and Peter on either side of me as the undertaker looked over to me to give the OK to go. I was rooted to the spot and in a kind of a twilight zone. I couldn't bring myself to say 'yes' or even to nod. Siobhán, who was with her friends, came over to me and said:

'We should go.'

'You tell him,' I said, 'I can't.' The funeral set out.

Siobhán drove me, Mary and Tom and Peter and Tony travelled together and we all followed the hearse. When eventually we arrived the parish priest preceded the coffin into the church and conducted the reception. He reminded me of Father Keane in my last parish. He was older, kindly and shook hands with each of us, none of whom he had met before. He had a firm handshake, looked me straight in the eye and said simply 'I'm sorry'. Siobhán and I sat in the front seat of the church and Kate's siblings and their families sat behind us. The priest conducted the reception with sensitivity and I assumed from a couple of things he said that he wasn't aware that Kate and I weren't married. Eamon said to me afterwards that he was surprised that Una hadn't told him. After the reception service there were a couple of decades of the rosary through which Siobhán and I sat in silence because neither of us knew it. Then the families went back to Eamon and Teresa's house for food and a drink. Both of Kate's sisters were solicitous of Siobhán and showed great interest in her nursing career. One of Una's daughters, who was there, was a nurse in Cork. I had been looking forward to meeting the nun, but she wasn't able to come until the following day.

'I'll make sure you meet her tomorrow,' Eamon said to me, 'although I doubt if there's any chance you'll miss her.'

If I thought that the whole community had turned out for the reception the night before, for the funeral there could have been only the bed-bound left at home. The church was packed and there were as many again outside. Kate's family was highly thought of, and people attend funerals as occasions to express their respect for families or in the hope there'll be a good crowd at their own, as much as to express their sympathy for the death.

Una's pious brother-in-law celebrated the mass and gave the homily. It was clear that *he* knew that Kate and I hadn't been married; he skirted around the matter. He made Siobhán the chief mourner and spoke about Kate's family in the community. At the graveside I received the handshakes of sympathy with the others and I was reminded of Jennifer's burial. As I stood there I realised that I was burying the third of the three women I had loved although I had lost touch for many years with Maura Murray by the time she had died.

I was a virtual cripple in the midst of a large crowd shaking hands with people I had never seen before in my life and almost all of whom I would never see again. I was bewildered to the point of wanting to run away, and might well have if I had been able. I wanted this ritual of 'sorry for your trouble' with these strangers to end and to go back to the house with Kate's family and mine. I was assailed again by the reality that I would spend the rest of my life on my own, which I never thought would happen. There would be no Kate, no more times when we would share our thoughts about all of the things that mattered to both of us; the intimate discussions about meaning and purpose, life and death and all the unanswered and unanswerable questions. Kate was gone and all I could salvage from that was that she had never avoided the mystery. She had learned to live with it. This was the basis of our love and respect for each other that in some small way gave to our lives some meaning. There was no one else with whom I could discuss, as we often did, what Brendan Kennelly identified in one of his poems as: '*the small protective sanities that hide men from themselves.*'

The graveside ritual eventually ended and we went back to Eamon and Teresa's. I wasn't in the door when the nun came over to me. She was a medical doctor and had spent years on the missions in Africa and claimed that she had learned as much, if not more, from the Africans as they had learned from her.

'John,' the nun said to me, 'she was great. She once told me how much you meant to her.' I could contain myself no longer. I cried. The nun helped me over to a sofa, sat beside me and held my hand while I collected myself. I could have shared anything with this beautiful person that the family demeaned by simply referring to her as the nun.

'I don't know what to call you,' I said.

'I'm Kathleen. I used to have a religious name but I don't use it anymore. I was called after a male medieval Italian saint. It was all nonsense, a device to depersonalise you, one of the many things designed to turn you into an obedient religious automaton that could be more easily controlled. I was baptised Kathleen and what's more appropriate for a holy nun than to use the Christian name her parents gave her.'

We sat and talked. She knew I had been a clergyman and we discovered that we had much in common. She did not give unqualified loyalty to anything, especially the Church. I could understand why Una never talked about her.

While we sat there entirely at ease in each other's company Eamon came over and spoke to Kathleen. It was clear that they were friends. He asked her if she would mind if he took me away for a while as he still hadn't done the herding.

'Good idea,' Kathleen said, 'some fresh air'll help to clear his head.' They helped me up and Eamon and I went through the kitchen out to the yard. After no little effort Eamon sat me up into the Land Rover and as we drove out of the yard he asked:

'Well, what did you make of all that?'

'Much as I expected,' I replied.

'What about our mother and father waiting at the Gates to greet Kate?' Eamon asked.

'When I did believe, more or less, that there might be a God and a heaven, I didn't believe that kind of thing. People who say it mean well, but it's the kind of nonsense that is said to comfort credulous people in their grief, to give them some hope or comfort in the face of death. The trouble is there's no comfort in the face of death. Death and bereavement are part of the natural order and we have to cope with them as best we can. Death is obscene – offensive to us. It's about loss and the best way to diminish loss is to be thankful for what went before.'

'John, I have to be honest, I never believed that kind of thing either, but when it comes from a priest it beats Banagher.'

'It's like this, Eamon: as I think you know I don't believe there's a God or a heaven at all and that makes a lot more sense to me than all the religion business.'

'If I knew a bit more and had time to think about these things, I have a feeling that that's where I'd end up too,' Eamon said, and we both fell silent. We were parked in a gateway and after a while Eamon went to look at the cattle. When he came back:

'I'm sure I told you before that I was ten years younger than Kate, and when I was small she used to look after me. She took mS side against the other two and she taught me a lot. She'd bring me for a walk and tell me about the trees and the wild flowers in the ditch. She had a book she sometimes brought and she'd look up a flower or a tree and put a name on it. She was great. I was bloody mad when Conor left her, but saving your presence she did better in the end. I couldn't say that to Una or Clare. Una would say that when you make your bed you have to lie in it.'

'Moral certainty is a sign of social insecurity,' I said, 'socially secure people say 'I think' and are prepared to say: 'I'm not sure or I don't know.' It's a sign of maturity to live easily with uncertainty and not to be threatened by diversity.'

'Begod John, that's very profound.'

'It's not a bit profound. The same sentiment is expressed commonly by 'live and let live'. Institutions demand loyalty and give security to their members. If you think outside the box you may have to end up living outside the institution. Having listened to

Kathleen I don't know how she's still inside the Church. Maybe she thinks she can be an influence for change if she stays in, but the institution will win in the end; you can't kick against the pricks. With her temperament, if she wants to be herself she'll have to leave, and I have a feeling she knows that.'

'It's hard to believe that Una and Clare are out of the same litter as Kate and me. It's a strange old world, John. It's a strange old world.'

When we arrived back at the house there were only a few cars in the yard. Later that evening Mary and Tom and Peter and Tony went back to Dublin. Siobhán cried a lot during the time of the funeral, but apart from that she kept her grief to herself. If she didn't talk about it, I would try in time to encourage her to do so. She and I stayed the night and left after breakfast in the morning. Siobhán, who had no contact with her father's family, talked about Eamon, Una and Clare and her cousins. They had all told her how much they would like to see more of her and she was resolved to take them at their word and to go and stay from time to time. Her candour surprised me when she said:

'I wonder how Una would take it if I arrived for the weekend with a partner?'

My not responding would leave the question in her mind that I might have reservations so I reassured her:

'In that case I think you'd be better to stay with Eamon and Teresa; I have a feeling it wouldn't be a bother to them.'

We talked about the changed circumstance for both of us. Kate had told us individually that she was leaving the house to Siobhán giving me right of residence for my lifetime.

'With just the two of us in the house, how do you think we'll manage?' I said. 'I don't want you to have to spend time doing things for me. You have your young life to lead.'

'I'll do what I can,' she said.

It was a strange sensation for both of us. Kate had been the common factor; domestic life had rotated around her. Siobhán and I were experiencing different kinds of grief, that of a daughter for her mother and of a partner for his beloved. We talked about Kate. The reality of having to make a new life dawned slowly. It would never be the same again for either of us. However, Siobhán was young and had an expanding life ahead of her. My life, with age and infirmity, was contracting.

Before she left the house every morning Siobhán brought me a mug of tea and left me to take my time getting up and dressed, which I could just about manage on my own. The most difficult thing was the stairs. When I arrived onto the ground floor I could manage most things slowly. I read, listened to radio and dozed on and off for much of the day. At about four o'clock I prepared vegetables and set the table for two in the kitchen. When Siobhán came in she did the rest. From time to time Siobhán took me out in the car.

'You'll have to get out of the house more or you'll go mad. It won't do you any good sitting at home. You won't live long if you loose touch with the world.'

'Sometimes it's not a great world to be in touch with,' I said, and knew that it was different for Siobhán.

One Friday night Siobhán announced that Clodagh, her platonic friend, as she called her, was coming around in the morning to help her to carry a single bed from the spare bedroom down to the sitting-room. We had talked about it a number of times. It would ease things greatly for me not to have to negotiate the stairs.

CHAPTER 11

One afternoon I had just finished the sandwich that Siobhán had left for my lunch when there was a ring at the door. By the time I arrived to open it there was nobody there. As I was closing it I happened to glance across and on the far side of the street, down a little way, I saw Bob Furney, the archdeacon in the last diocese where I had served, about to get into his car. I called. He heard me and came back:

'Hello John, I thought there was nobody in.'

'Come in, Bob, it's good to see you. The first door there.' I followed him in. 'This room is where I 'live and move and have my being' these days. Would you ever throw the cover up on the bed; I don't have many visitors and I don't always make it.' Bob put the cover up and sat down.

'Well John, how are things? Haven't seen you for years.'

'I'm riddled with arthritis and getting around is a problem. It's mainly my back and my legs, but it's everywhere. It's a bugger.' I held out my hands to show him the distortion of my fingers that made holding or manipulating anything difficult.

'What about pain?'

'It's shocking. I take powerful pain-killers but they do a terrible job on my stomach and I have to take something to counter that. If I develop side-effects from that, they'll probably give me something to counter those side-effects and so on *ad nauseam!* If you know what I mean? No, I jest, for the moment I can cope. My best hope, they tell me, is that in time the pain might diminish and go altogether. It may burn itself out. I'd settle for that, but the doctor doesn't know if this'll happen and since other systems are starting to break down, I mightn't last long enough. Anyway you didn't come to hear an earful about my infirmities.'

'I came to say how sorry I was to hear that your wife had died.'

'Kate and I weren't married, Bob. We saw no reason to, and we were closer and happier than many a man and wife.'

'I'm delighted to hear it, but that makes it all the harder for you.'

'We had such good years together I'm very grateful. It takes time to come to terms with being on my own. I live with Kate's daughter Siobhán who's a nurse. She's good to me, but I'm determined that she won't have to nurse me. She has a life of her own.'

I hadn't known Bob well; he was at the other end of the diocese from me, but we met from time to time at events. He had always struck me as an open and honest man. He wasn't a career cleric, so there was great surprise and no little bitching amongst the clergy when the bishop appointed him archdeacon.

'John, I have to tell you that I often meant to contact you to have a chat, and when I heard of your bereavement it was the stimulus to come.'

'I'm glad to see you. I have had almost no contact with former colleagues. I often wonder what they thought of my leaving.'

'I've never heard it discussed, but then I'm not on the inside track in clerical circles. The only reaction I ever heard was early on from the bishop: he told me he was sad that you left. The thing is John that I struggle with believing a lot of things myself.'

I waited for Bob to go on. There was a long silence. Then he said:

'Would you mind telling me the things that caused you to leave?'

'Certainly. I don't bring it up unless people ask me questions, when I am perfectly happy to answer them and discuss these matters if they want to. I'll tell you the kinds of thing that finally tipped me over so that I couldn't stay. It's a long story, but stop me if you want to. Before I tell you of my own experience I should tell you what I think belief and religion are, and about the effect that they have.

'There is a dimension to human experience that is not scientific, empirical or material. Perhaps the most universal and mysterious of all such is the example of 'falling in love'. You may believe from their behaviour that a person is in love, but you can't prove it scientifically. It's something that's going on inside the person's head and heart. I believe that belief in a god is something like that; not amenable to scientific proof, but real none the less for the person who believes, and having no reality outside the person experiencing it.

'I believe religion is an emotional psychological device to give some security and hope to enable people to survive in this unfathomable, painful, unjust and mysterious world. When evolution arrived at the point that the species was able to reflect on its condition, to make itself the object of its own thought, I believe it invented a god to try and make some sense of its precarious predicament. They constructed a god they could appease and please in order that he would grant the right conditions for their material survival, sun and rain at the right times. By the way, some farmers today haven't moved far from that. Tribal gurus arose who claimed to have special insights and influence with this god and became tribal priests. This perceived influence put them in positions of power with the ordinary people. These tribal priests then built around their status all kinds of control in matters that became sin and salvation and they invented tribal rituals which they controlled in order to exercise power over the ordinary members of the tribe.

'This all then evolved into the religious issues of Christian history. Denial of, or even dissent from, the tribal religion meant death, and when the truths of one Christian tribe were in conflict with the truths of another Christian tribe they went to war and slaughtered each other in the name of the God of love they claimed to believe in. During the course of history religious belief became one of the most common sources of hatred in the world and all that follows from hatred. You only have to pick up a newspaper to see that is still the case.

'The first thing I have to say about myself is that I was always by temperament a sceptic. I often told parishioners that if there's no doubt there's no faith. Doubt is the corollary of faith and if you can believe what Jesus is reported to have said on the cross: "my God, my God why hast thou forsaken me?" he too had doubts. I never really understood why, as some people believe and the Church teaches, a universal God would set up a system to test people so that some would be rewarded by some kind of eternal life and others would be punished with eternal damnation. For that's what any doctrine of salvation is about no matter how watered down it is these days. I found a lot of things difficult to believe: the virgin birth, miracles, resurrection and a whole lot more. I put them on the back burner because I loved working with people in the parish, as I saw it, creating community and conducting ritual to try to help people to cope with life. From time to time, inexplicably, something would turn up the heat that would cause the questions on the back burner to boil over and I'd go through agonies as to whether I should leave. There weren't any easy options to turn to; I would have had to train from scratch at something else. Then the work in the parish would take over again and what I considered my own oddity faded until the next time. Eventually I had such a conscience about my doubts that I went to the bishop, told him what I didn't believe and he didn't really take me seriously. He said it was just a phase, it'll pass, have a holiday, it's a grief reaction after Jennifer's death, he was pleasant, but hopeless, so I pulled out. That's it in a nutshell'

'You said you often wondered what some of the others thought of you leaving. You won't mind if I tell you.'

'Not in the slightest. What other people think doesn't bother me, however, go ahead.'

'It's all water under the bridge now, but at the time, and probably still, if they were asked, people would say it was because you were having an affair and you had to go.' I didn't respond for a minute in order to take this in, then:

'I'm staggered. I'm staggered; it never occurred to me. Kate and I didn't become lovers until after I had been to the bishop and had decided to leave. She had been a good friend to Jennifer and she and I did what we could to help her, but failed. Kate was a good friend to both of us, but there was nothing romantic between us until some time after Jennifer died; after I had made up my mind that I had to leave because I just didn't believe the stuff. Kate was a deserted wife for quite a while and I was a widower. Would you say that was an affair? I suppose I can't blame people; we became romantically attached before I actually left the parish, but not before I had made up my mind to leave the ministry.'

'I suppose too that it made people feel better that you left because of an affair, than that you left because you lost the faith.'

'Bob, I didn't lose the faith. I left because I made a conscious and carefully arrived at decision that I didn't believe the essential doctrines of the Christian religion any more.'

'If it ever arises again, have I your permission to tell people that?'

'I don't mean to give you a short answer, but you can tell people whatever you like. It's irrelevant to me what they think.'

'If it does arise, I think it's only fair to you if I put the record straight.'

'Strangely enough it wasn't difficulty with the virgin birth, the resurrection, the divinity of Christ or any of those things that finally tipped me over. They had always been a problem and they certainly contributed. No. The final straw was that I was reading something about the universe. Science was never my thing at school. In fact I swapped it for Latin when I couldn't work out why they were making such a big deal about the Bunsen burner. However I look things up occasionally. Do you know the size of the universe? These figures are etched in my mind: the universe is 90 billion light years across and one light year is about six trillion miles. Work that one out, and it's about fourteen billion years old. We cannot conceive of its immensity and there's no language that can help us to describe it apart from statistics and they're unfathomable. Earth is one small planet in a solar system in the Milky Way galaxy, and the Milky Way is more than 100,000 light years in diameter which has as many as 400 billion stars. Now wait for it: scientists tell us that there are as many galaxies in the universe as there are grains of sand in every desert in the world! Scientists don't know if there is life as we know it anywhere else in the universe. Some think there can't be and some believe that it's possible that there is. You may think I'm a bit of a statistician, but I memorised all these figures so staggered was I by them, though some of them may be out by a mile or two!'

'Good grief,' said Bob, and before he could say anything else I went on:

'And what's more the scientists tell us now there may be other universes than ours. As Paddy, who used to help me with the garden at the rectory, would say when he had just passed on the latest piece of local scandal: "Merciful hour and His Blessed Mother your reverence, what do you think o' that?" Now, Bob, before I tell you the rest, how about a cup of tea or coffee? The only thing is, if you'd like it sometime in the near future you'll have to make it yourself.'

'No thanks; I had lunch just before I came.'

'That doesn't preclude a cup of tea or coffee.'

'No thanks, I'm fine.'

'Would you like me to go on?'

'If you don't mind.'

'Well stop me anytime you like. The question is as you can see, why would a God, if there were one, create all of this and set up the evolution of our species to test them out on one tiny insignificant planet in the middle of nowhere? You see that's the point. We're here because earth was just the right distance from the sun, not too close, not too far, to allow our species to evolve and when the species came to the point of asking themselves how they arrived here and what it was all about they had no science as we know it so they invented a god to account for it and I believe that that was how religion started.

'Then you'll be familiar with the other big problem I had. If there were a good all powerful, all merciful, all loving God, as the Church teaches, why would he allow so much evil and so much pain and suffering in the world. The old theodicy problem. In my opinion nobody in the history of the Church that I know of has answered it satisfactorily, and as far as I can remember it was never mentioned in Divinity School. They didn't talk about the Holocaust, world starvation, babies born with cancer and I needn't tell you the rest. You know it all yourself.

'Add to these kinds of questions the problems of theology: virgin birth, resurrection, miracles and so on; the evil perpetrated by religion; burning people who didn't agree with you, religious wars, the subjugation of women and I could go on and on. For me the scientific account of why and how we're here makes sense and religion, most of which comes from a pre-scientific age, does not. Religion became a power and control issue and human beings are obsessed with power and control of other human beings, and what better way to bring people under your control than to claim that you have the power to offer them the reward of heaven and to enable them to avoid the eternal punishment of hell. Religion uses the innate fear of death to offer eternal life if you do what I tell you; faith not science or reason will save you. Well Bob, I found I could no longer believe that and came to the conclusion that I believed that there was no God and I have been happy with that ever since. Nobody knows, or can prove if there is a God or not and I believe firmly that there isn't. The tradition into which we were both born comforts itself that the authority on which it bases what it teaches as the truth is threefold: scripture, tradition and reason. For me, given modern biblical studies, scripture creates more problems than it answers, tradition much the same and as far as I'm concerned these days reason comes down firmly on 'no God' so that's why I am where I am, and happy to be here. I can live with myself now in a way I could never do when I was in the Church.'

'Well, well, John, you have it all worked out. You had all the same kind of problems that I have and a few more besides. Do you mind if I ask you a few questions?'

'Ask me anything in the world you like except about my sex life which I can assure you these days is entirely defunct!'

'What about Jesus?'

'Well first of all, the picture we have of Jesus is almost entirely from the gospels and you know as well as I do the background to the writing of the gospels. They weren't just historical accounts of events. They were written well after the events and were written to portray Jesus as the person the writers wanted him to be. As you know too it was not uncommon for people in those days to believe that exceptional and notable individuals were gods. The Roman Emperor for example and there were other teachers around the Middle East at the same time as Jesus, but their divinity didn't survive. Even the Japanese emperor in our own time is believed to be a god in some sense, not I think that the Japanese believe he created the universe, and they know that he gets sick and needs a doctor from time to time, so as a deity he's not quite the full shilling. I don't know how all that's supposed to work, but back to Jesus. Am I teaching my granny to suck eggs?'

'In a way yes, but I'd like to hear how you put it all together.'

'I don't put it all together in any kind of a fully coherent way, but if it doesn't sound arrogant, over the years I have developed views on most of these things. Jesus, yes Jesus. He was simply a remarkable human being but was well presented and promoted as God by the power-brokers of the early Church and when

Constantine adopted Christianity as the religion of the Empire Jesus really took off. Christianity became compulsory and when anybody had the temerity to question it or to dissent from it they were executed, ultimately by the Church who claimed to be the presence of Christ in the world. They tortured and executed people in the name of the Prince of Peace who taught that they should love their enemies, forgive seventy times seven, turn the other cheek. Bob, it just didn't make sense to me. Although Christianity is more benign today, there are so many varieties of it and they all believe the other ones are wrong. If you listen to the incredible nonsense that some of them believe it would blow your mind. At least science is credible and provable and can be shown to work and where it is disproved it is discarded by the scientific method. It has integrity. As far as I'm concerned the authority of not just Christianity but of all religions doesn't have integrity. When they come to the real problems they don't address them seriously, they say you must have faith.'

'But what about the Jesus that people say they have taken into their lives and have a personal relationship with who has turned their lives around and has given their lives meaning? We've both seen it happen.'

'Yes, people for whom it has happened have told me about it. It never happened to me. They attribute the experience to Jesus. People brought up in other religions attribute the same kind of experience to Allah or Krishna or whoever their god is. This makes me believe that these experiences are universal human experiences. To put it simply, they take place inside people's heads. They are some kind of emotional dependent experiences that people who have them attribute to the god or prophet of the religious culture they were brought up in. I believe that these are purely subjective human experiences that take place inside the human organism and have nothing to do with a transcendent god. People have had the same conversion experiences to Communism and Nazism and many other 'isms' no doubt, without any claim that they have their origin in a god of any kind, and you know where those two led. They all have one thing in common: they require the suspension of reason and the rule of the emotions. They give a purpose and meaning to meaningless lives. They give certainty to people in confusion and require mindless adherence to one kind of philosophy or other that gives security to the individual. As I say, you know where commitment to Communism and Nazism led. In the past, similar commitment to religions led to people being burned at the stake, and to the slaughter of thousands and thousands of people in religious wars. In recent times we had the same in Northern Ireland, Protestants killing Catholics and vice versa for no other reason than that they subscribed to the other version of the same religion. Exactly the same happens between Sunni and Shia and between Muslims and Christians. All wars are venomous, vicious and evil, and all wars are fought in the name of some 'ism' secular or religious and don't forget that even democracy is an 'ism'. It may be the best we have or it may not. Democracy and Christianity are the ones we were brought up in but neither of them is beyond criticism.

'It requires only one thing for people to believe the most incredible fantasy and that is that people should suspend their reason. If you suspend your reason there is no end to what you can believe. When the fundamental doctrines of Christianity were laid down as 'gospel' if you know what I mean, some of the brightest minds around based them on emotion, political expediency and probably many other things that were not amenable to reason. These doctrines are immutable and still subscribed to by the Church. Yes some of the finest theological minds around today have tried to reconcile these doctrines of a time before science to the twenty-first century, but you'd need a brain like these theologians to understand them and the punter in the pew certainly doesn't. The punter in the pew sees belief in simplistic terms that are at base loyalty to the tradition in which they were brought up. How many people convert from one religion to another based on the exercise of their reason? A tiny, tiny number and they often become bigots with the zeal of the newly-converted. The rest go to any lengths of one kind or another in defence of the religion in which they were brought up.

'As I said, when you suspend your reason, you can believe anything. The doctrines of the Church are incredible and require just that, that you suspend your reason. The Church says piously: 'reason can bring you only so far and then you need faith.' Why? Why not base what we believe on reason alone because when you enter the realm of faith anything goes? How Pope John Paul II could have believed that the assassin's bullet was deflected by the Virgin Mary so that it only injured him rather than killing him. I find it incredible that a highly intelligent educated man like John Paul II could believe that kind of nonsense. In the realm of this kind of fantasy if the Virgin could deflect a bullet would she not have been better to have paralysed the assassin's arm so that he could not have fired the gun in the first place and saved the Pope injury. By the way, how anyone can believe that the mother of Jesus could have entered heaven, a spiritual realm, in her human body without decay, based on an Old Testament verse "My holy one shall not see corruption" I don't know. More fantasy. Limbo was fantasy and they abolished that; maybe they'll abolish a few more incredible doctrines when they reflect on what fantasy they expect intelligent educated people to believe these days. Protestants are no better when they use the Bible as some kind of infallible authority to justify the most amazing things. As you know not all Protestants are fundamentalists but even those that aren't use the authority of the Bible to justify beliefs that I could no longer subscribe to.

'I may be wrong about all of these things, but I have only one life to live and, like Frank Sinatra, "I'll do it my way." Why? Because I don't believe most of the speculation and superstition that passes for truth as taught by the Church. I prefer reason and science for what I believe. It's simply not possible to prove one way or another whether there is a God or not. I don't *know* that there is no God, but it is reasonable to say I *believe* that there isn't, because that's the conclusion that my reason brings me to, in exactly the same way that suspending their reason brings believing Christians to the belief that there is.

'Believing Christians depend on the Church, theologians and cognoscenti for what they believe. I depend on scientists for what I believe, and to put it simply I prefer to depend on scientists than on theologians. Unlike the Church, science makes a virtue of scepticism and scepticism is a useful tool as we look for the truth. I depend every day on what scientists have discovered. If I become ill I go to the doctor who relies almost entirely on science to cure me. If I want to go to New York I'm quite happy to fly in a jetliner that is the product of science. I trust these and many other similar things over against the things that theologians tell me – that a God impregnated a virgin in order to arrive on this speck of a speck of a planet in the unfathomable immensity of the universe. That he rose from the dead, that he's ensconced in some spiritual realm observing all the pain and suffering in the world and doing nothing about it, even though as God if he were merciful he could do something about it. That he'll come a second time, this time in glory, and wind the whole thing up. Then he'll sort out the "goodies" from the "baddies" amongst everybody who has ever lived, of whatever religion, and those still alive. I have no doubt which of the two options, science or theology makes the more sense to me.

'Bob, why didn't you stop me? I've never put it all together in one diatribe like that before, but you did ask! I know that lots of the things I've said are debatable, but what I've told you is where I'm content to be. It's the best I can do. I believe that one of the most important things any of us can do is to make up our own minds. Listen to what the institutions and the philosophies say, in so far as you can understand them, listen to what other people say, but don't abdicate to other people what you believe. The most important thing that parents can teach their children, as Kate used to say, is to make up their own minds. It's hard, however, because the Church indoctrinates children from an early age when they're like blotting paper and absorb what authority figures tell them. So effective is this indoctrination, especially when it's laced with guilt and fear, that it is almost indelible. When the child comes to adulthood and begins to think for himself or herself the childhood indoctrination hasn't gone away. Deep down they say: "it doesn't all add up to me, but what, if despite everything, it's true? I'd better hang in there just in case."'

'I did ask you John, and I'm fascinated by all you've said. Most, but not all, of it in one form or another I have struggled with myself over the years.'

'Well, Bob, when I come to cock the toes I'll have the satisfaction of knowing that I did my best to be honest with myself and if I have been wrong, so be it. You know that TV programme where the presenter discuses with notable people what they believe? You know the interviewer's last question is always about what if orthodox Church teaching is right after all and when the subjects die they arrive at the pearly gates and are confronted by God, what will they say to him? I have put that question to myself and I have a lot of things I'd say; I'd take up a good bit of his time and it would be mostly questions:

"Why the hell did you not make it unequivocally clear that you existed and what you were about? How could you have sat up here and allowed such evil and suffering to afflict so many people in the world and lived up to your reputation as a loving God? For instance how could you have watched Hitler and Stalin do their worst and not have stopped them? Why did you allow earthquakes and tsunamis to kill hundreds of thousands of people and leave millions of people living in misery? You can't blame that on the badness or wilfulness of humans as they exercised their free will if they had any. That must be somebody else's fault! Why did you set up such a vast universe? One galaxy or one solar system or even one planet would have been enough for your purposes. Why, if Jesus was really you, did you go to only one small area and group of people in the Middle East? You must have known that most of the world had little or no chance of hearing about him from there; the Chinese, the Indians the Arabs, three quarters or more of the world and what about the indigenous peoples of America and Australia? Was it fair not to let them know? To have relied on missionaries in due course was a ridiculous way of letting them know about you."

'By the time I'd finished I believe that, if he were the right man, in other words if he was the God who started it all, he'd understand perfectly well where I was coming from and he'd probably say something like: "If I try anything like that again I'll give you a shout and maybe you'll help me to get it right next time."'

Bob came in:

'Seriously, John, I don't think I ever believed in life after death. Although the Church teaches it and over the years I took dozens of funerals I was never convinced that there is anything after we die.

Clergy who no longer believe in life after death become functionaries of an institution with aspirations in which they no longer have confidence. I've talked to lay people who doubt it too but still go to church every Sunday. There's more to religion than beliefs: as you know there's ritual and community, and both play an important part in people's lives. Did you miss either of those when you left the Church?'

'To be honest, Bob, I didn't. But you're right. They say that the things that former Christians who become atheist miss are those two: ritual and community, and they're connected. Communities have rituals of one kind or another and in our culture until recently most of them were centred on the Church. I have my own little rituals: when I was able, it was a ritual of mine to bring Kate a mug of tea in bed first thing. It was a ritual to look out the window while I shaved, to walk on the beach and buy the newspapers on Sundays. Private and secular sanities perhaps, as the poet said, to hide me from myself. I was never comfortable with public and community events, but many people seem to need them. Atheists and humanists meet and talk, but they don't have ritual or community events. In fact there have always been atheists, but for many of them it was just a fact that they saw no reason to discuss with other people. They had no inclination to commune with other atheists. I don't seem to have a need of formal ritual or of public community; family and friends are important, but not the public at large.

'When religion was triumphant and ran the show in this country, to be an atheist was to be a pariah. All that has changed as you know and the young people vote with their feet. The Churches are having to adjust to the fact that not everybody believes there is a God.'

'John, I've taken up enough of your time. It's been good to talk to you.'

'It's been good for me too, Bob. Don't hesitate to come if you would like to talk again. To be honest the biggest mystery to me is why so many of the clergy don't appear to have more problems of belief. Maybe they do but don't do anything about their doubts. I suspect that some of the clergy are in fact atheist but they're not motivated to do anything about it for one reason or another.'

Bob didn't respond, but we chatted on about this and that for quite a time. He brought me up to date about what was going on in the diocese, then he stood up, and said:

'Thank you again. All that's been very interesting. Don't even get up; I'll see myself out.'

CHAPTER 12

Around this time I worried constantly about where I was going, or rather what would happen to me. I wasn't 'going' anywhere; I would have to be brought. I wasn't in the slightest worried about dying, though as yet, obviously, for myself, I had addressed the issue only theoretically. I had been brought up with a great sense of right and wrong, but even in my most religious phase I had had no sense of a heaven and hell. Right and wrong were about here and now. The doctor assured me that he had no reason to believe that I would die in the near future, but one never knows. I was becoming less able to do things for myself. The problem was that I would become even more crippled and more dependent on somebody to look after me. When doing those things that I could still do I was becoming slower and slower. I was concerned that I should not be a damned nuisance to Siobhán. I was determined not to impose on her in my decrepitude. Siobhán reassured me:

'I'm glad you're in the house. It's a great security; I wouldn't like to live alone, and you're a great help preparing the vegetables and loading the dishwasher.' I was grateful for Siobhán's assurance that she was glad I was in the house and although I had a legal right to be there I wasn't sure in my own mind that I had a moral right. There was a sense that Kate and Siobhán had taken me in, but I had no doubt that neither of them ever saw it that way. I would not have liked to have had to live with Mary, not that I could, nor indeed that she would have agreed to such an arrangement. If it came to it I think Peter and I could have made some fist of living together and Tony would be kind. It was inevitable that the time would come that I would have to be taken in somewhere and looked after.

One day, out of the blue, the local rector called. I had not had any contact with the local parish and didn't even know who the rector was. He was a couple of generations younger than me. I thought immediately that Bob had said something to someone who had drawn the wrong conclusion, but no, the rector told me a woman, whose name I didn't know, had told him I was living in his parish. He was a pleasant enough young man, but I didn't want him to be under any illusion about where I stood:

'Yes, I spent quite a long time in the ministry of the Church, but I have been an atheist now for many years.' I didn't want to be too blunt with him, but it soon became clear to me that he was of the evangelical school and very religious.

'I understand,' he said, 'can I tell you where I stand?' and without waiting for a reply from me he launched into a long story about how he had been wayward as a youth but had met Jesus and had given his life to the Lord. I'd heard it all before. Even when I did believe I didn't believe the kind of thing he was recounting. I didn't want to offend him, but I wasn't in the slightest interested in what he was saying. I didn't want him to come back again. I had no doubt that he had a list of people he had saved and would have considered a former clergyman who became atheist quite a scalp to add to his collection.

'I don't think there is any point in us discussing these things,' I said, 'we're poles apart and I have no doubt that we won't find common ground. You're good to call, and you're welcome to stay as long as you don't talk about religion.'

He didn't respond and I jumped in quickly with:

'Do you follow rugby?'

'No, I'm not interested in sport.'

'What about politics?'

'I'm not interested in politics either.'

'What are you interested in?'

'The only thing that really interests me is my work for the Lord,' and he stood up.

'Thank you for coming,' I said, 'can I ask you to let yourself out; the less walking I have to do the better.'

'I'll pray for you ….I'm sorry, I didn't get your name?'

'John.'

'John.'

'And I didn't get your name.'

'Brian.'

'I'm sorry, Brian, I should have offered you a cup of coffee.'

'Thanks, all the same, I don't drink coffee.'

'I'm sorry I can't shake hands with you; you can see the state of my fingers.'

'Don't worry,' he said, and went.

'Every cripple has his own way of walking,' I thought, 'and we're all cripples.'

There was a sense in which I respected his patent sincerity, while disagreeing entirely with what he understood that life was about. He seemed to me to make the mistake that many people make; he believed that truth was easily known. He had a simple straightforward belief that gave him purpose and meaning, and his mission in life was to persuade as many people as possible to come to the same belief.

I had no right to believe that my understanding of what I was doing when I was in the ministry had been the right one. Of course I knew there were other understandings of what a clergyman should be about, like Brian and many others who used the Bible as a handbook for what they saw as the necessity of the traditional religious version of salvation. Then there were the High Church ones for whom the sacraments were almost a mechanical means of grace. I was never quite sure what grace was or even what a soul was. It seemed that the soul was part of a person that survived physical death. I remember a philosophy lecturer in college who posed the question as to when you had listed all the chemical components of the human body was there anything else, and of course there is. There is the unique person; how they walk and talk, the part that loves and forgives or hates or is vindictive and so on and on. This lecturer left us to work out the implications of this for ourselves. However he wasn't hinting at a soul for he had made it clear earlier on that he was an atheist. This allowed some of my fellow divinity students to discount everything he said. One of them said to me after that lecture:

'How can he not see that that's the soul?'

'Maybe it's just the personality,' I said, and we launched into a long discussion about what was psychological and what was spiritual. I didn't argue, because I didn't know. When I was in college all this kind of stuff was new to me. Some of my evangelical colleagues had all the answers and were certain about everything because they had it in the Bible, at least the bits of the Bible they wanted to use to buttress the case that some kind of a conversion experience had given them. What they did with the rest of the Bible, the bits that didn't add up or were contrary to what they believed, I didn't know. Perhaps I did know really. The bits they couldn't reconcile to their point of view they simply ignored.

For me the task was to help people away from meaninglessness by giving a purpose to life through family and community by means of a sound ethic and the use of ritual. That for me was salvation; saving people from lack of purpose or meaning. It wasn't saving people from the power and penalty of sin, especially reward or punishment after death. Salvation wasn't achieving eternal happiness. It was about here and now because as I thought about the history of the world and the evolution of the species, I saw a version of purpose and meaning being pedalled by religion that had been constructed by humankind before we had any knowledge of evolution. This version of religion led eventually to bitterness, hatred, injustice and even slaughter. I believed that all we could salvage from the mess was to accept the reality of human nature with all its flaws, behave towards each other with a reasonable and honourable ethic that was based on love and forgiveness and live until we die. For me the ethic of Jesus was as good as any, though it wasn't all original to him. The best we can do is to live by the golden rule: do unto others as you would they should do unto you, love your neighbour as yourself, which of course is impossible to do but a good goal to strive towards, and forgive seventy times seven, not impossible but rare. Somebody said that life was an exercise in forgiveness. I had no view on the great imponderables other than to accept that they were part of the human condition. The great imponderables to me were the existence of evil; man's inhumanity to man, and even more so man's inhumanity to woman, physical flaws and deformities even in newborn babies, inequality and lack of justice in the society and in the world at large; people dying of hunger in the third world while people were dying of obesity in the first world. All we can do is to organise ourselves and society as best we can to alleviate these things as much as we are able. It is difficult to alleviate more than a small amount compared to the immensity of the problem, but as the aphorism says: it's better to light a candle than to curse the dark.

I was perfectly content with what I believed myself. I didn't seem to need what people called the comforts of religion. Over the years, however, I had met people who had serious doubts or didn't believe at all, who envied those who did believe. They thought it must have been a wonderful comfort and assurance to believe the kind of thing that Brian believed. After he had called I began to wonder. I began to speculate what it might be like to have his kind of assurance that despite all the unanswered questions of life, despite the pain and suffering in the world, despite all, everything would be all right in the end. That is, as he said, if you gave your life to Jesus, and behaved moderately well here on earth you'd end up in eternal bliss. I tried to think myself into believing that kind of thing since at one level if it would solve all my problems it was an attractive proposition. Solving all my problems here and now was the attraction, not the eternal bliss bit; I had no fear or even aversion to extinction. In fact to live for ever in any realm held no appeal for me.

About two weeks after Brian had called, he called again. The first time I hadn't wanted to air all my opinions on religion, and faith. He was young and strongly committed to one way of believing. I was old and didn't believe. I didn't want to upset him. I had no right to tumble his castle. Not that I could; he was unshakeable in his beliefs. Like so many people of his kind he didn't 'believe', he 'knew'. This time I thought I'd throw the book at him. I gave him in great detail every possible reason for not believing in God. He listened and when I had finished he gave me answers to refute all my objections. They were simple and direct answers that required blind faith and he had a biblical text to back up all of them. What if he was right? I suspended my reason and allowed myself to enter his world; the world that was based on his assumptions and beliefs and found that it was a comforting place to be. It was, I speculated, what it was like to be on drugs. It was a mental and emotional state in which all my problems about believing fell away and didn't seem to matter. I experienced a warm secure feeling of wellbeing. I suspected that it was like drugs too in that it would wear off unless I had regular shots of it. It would need a regular dose of evangelical preaching to maintain the intensity of the experience for which I would need to go to the kind of church that Judy and Siobhán once went to. I gave in to the feeling and bathed my feet in the warmth and then suddenly he stood up and said he had to go; he was late for an appointment.

'Would you like me to call again?' he asked. If he had asked me that question at the end of his first visit, I'd have said 'no thank you'; but this time I said: 'yes drop in sometime when you have time.'

'Would you like me to say a prayer with you before I go?'

'Not this time, but come again.'

I began to wonder if I nurtured this kind of religion and allowed it to take me over, would it solve, or even make irrelevant, the problems that I knew lay ahead of me. I knew I would have to leave Siobhán's house and be taken in somewhere that people would look after me when I was able to do little or nothing for myself. With my emotions I had the feeling that the source of what I felt was God, but with my mind I knew that that couldn't be because I didn't believe a God existed. What if I was wrong and this was him giving me a final chance?

I did nothing to nurture this feeling. If there was a Bible in the house I wouldn't know where to find it, and if I did know I probably wouldn't have been able to reach it. Furthermore I wouldn't know where to find the appropriate texts. People nurture this feeling by consorting with like-minded people who believe the same kind of thing and they encourage each other in everything necessary to affirm it. I suppose that everybody who practises any kind of religion does that to some degree. I had no doubt that I would need to modify my rational approach and correct the imbalance between the cerebral and the emotional, but this was a case of going to the other extreme and suspending my reason almost entirely and allowing my emotions to take over. I couldn't bring myself to do that.

As my life ground slowly and inexorably on, that brief interlude faded and I saw it for what I knew it to be. It was a religious experience that its adherents believed had its origin in God. Those who embraced it were able to authenticate it to their own satisfaction by giving to the Bible a simplistic kind of authority and using it in an uncritical way. Having returned to what for me was normality I had no doubt that it was simply a psychological state with no transcendent source. It was something to do with dependence that psychologists could probably readily account for. The nature of this kind of experience will probably become clearer as today's great issue of science, the study of the mind, and in particular consciousness, progresses. I have no idea what all that is about: the question 'what is consciousness?' or trying to understand its structure. I didn't need to know and if somebody tried to explain it to me I probably wouldn't have been be able to understand it. I comforted myself that so long as somebody understood the principles I didn't need to. I didn't need to know the principles of the internal combustion engine to drive a car. I didn't need to know how to fly a jet airliner so long as the pilot did.

I had come to the conclusion that there is so much in life that any of us doesn't know that we have to leave a lot of things to other people. I felt strongly that that did not absolve me from making up my own mind on some questions, especially on the existence of God; was there one or not? With the limited knowledge and understanding that I had, relative to the religious and theological gurus of one kind or another, I came down firmly on the side of believing that there was no God and I was perfectly happy and content with that.

The time was approaching fast when I knew I could no longer be dependent on Siobhán. I had broached the subject with her from time to time, always with the same result. She would brush me off with excuses of one kind or another, some of which purported to show that my being in the house was a great help to her. Soon I would no longer be able to prepare the vegetables and it was taking me about quarter of an hour to finish packing the dishwasher and setting it off.

I knew that on balance I was more trouble than I was a help. Shaving was a trial so I skipped days and I wasn't able to wash properly. I was afraid that I would start to smell. I knew it was time to leave and find somewhere that I would have full-time care. Siobhán was looking after patients during her working day and she ought not to have to care for another when she came home.

CHAPTER 13

Peter and Tony came to see me every Saturday morning at about eleven o'clock. They always brought something; scones that were often still warm, a home-baked brack or a pot of home-made jam. As soon as they arrived Peter would make my bed and Tony would tidy the room. Siobhán would make posh coffee on her coffee machine that I wouldn't dare to touch, the machine that is, and the four of us would sit and chat. These Saturday mornings became a ritual that I came to value greatly.

Mary came from time to time, usually on a weekday evening. Tom and she had no children and both worked in Tom's business. They played golf and travelled when they could. I was never quite sure what kind of a marriage they had, but it seemed to hold together. I don't think Mary ever quite forgave Jennifer since she had first learned about her drinking.

It was clear that Peter and Tony enjoyed the Saturday mornings too. Peter loved to talk about the past and the way things were in 'the old days.' What Mary or Peter thought about religion I had no idea. I never broached the subject with either of them. They were their own people, but I suspected that Peter had been an atheist long before I was.

Having told Mary one evening that I could no longer stay with Siobhán, she took responsibility for finding somewhere that I could go. Now since I was no longer a clergyman, I would not have liked cynically to exploit some of the advantages of having been one, and there weren't many of those. There was an old people's home that had some kind of connection with the Church. I had never quite known what that connection was, but I did know that there were a number of retired clergy and clergy widows there. Each person had a room of their own and the good thing about it was that it had an infirmary, so that if an inmate became ill they would be looked after. If they had to go to hospital they would return to the infirmary after they had been discharged and if they had recovered well enough they could return to their room. This was a great attraction to me, as I didn't want to be shipped out to some other kind of hospital or nursing home in a state of terminal decline. One more move was as much as I wanted to have to make.

Mary asked the home if they would send me an application form. One of the questions asked me to state my occupation. I thought of putting 'Defunct Cleric', the term I used humorously to refer to myself, and see what they would make of that. I thought however that it mightn't encourage them to take me. I thought of putting: 'Retired Warehouseman', but since some people had an undue regard for the clergy, that would have lost me the advantage of having once been a member of that august body. To be straight with them I put: 'Former clergyman and retired warehouseman'. That was an honest description and I didn't say more than that about my track record. Whoever processed the form would probably know of me anyway and if they didn't it wouldn't be long before some earnest layman on the committee would tell them. Another question asked: 'Parish; name and address of rector'. I gave the name of Brian's parish and his address. I assumed that they would contact him and ask him whatever it was they wanted to know in order to evaluate whether I was a suitable specimen to admit or not.

I didn't tell Siobhán that I had submitted an application until I had done it.

'I know how you feel', she said, 'but as you know not only have you a legal right to stay, as far as I'm concerned you are welcome to. You're really not much of a nuisance and despite everything I'd miss you. After all you are the closest thing I've had to a father. Yes, I've met the man who was my biological father but you have put in the hours; you've done the hard slog over the years and I know that sometimes it wasn't easy and I'm grateful to you for everything you did for me, and for Kate too to help her to be a good Mum.' She paused, and I could see that she was moved. She went on: 'Enough of that old sentiment, but I've wanted to say that to you for a while and there it is. If you're determined to go you know well I can't stop you.'

'I am determined because it's the right thing for both of us.'

'Well I'll do what I can to help. When will you know if they'll have you?'

'I've no idea, I don't want to hassle them. If I haven't heard in a couple of months I'll ask Mary to phone.'

Some weeks after I had sent in the application Brian called.

'You gave my name as your rector on an application and they've sent me this form to fill in, but I have a problem.'

'I'd hate to cause you a problem.'

'The first question asks how long you have been a parishioner.'

'Brian, there is no problem. You know as well as I do that the answer to that question is something like: "He is not a parishioner. He lives in this parish and is known to me." I have nothing to hide and if I had, given the people who run that home, it would be impossible for me to conceal it.'

Brian went through the rest of the questions on the form and, prompted by me, he answered them without sinning his soul.

'All this would be a lot easier if you'd return to the flock.'

'And there'd be "rejoicing in heaven over the return of the one sheep that was lost and is found." Well, Brian, it's like this: if I were to do that I wouldn't be found, I'd be lost to all I believe strongly about life, religion and the whole caboodle and if there were a God, which as you know I don't believe there is, I don't believe he'd have much respect for me.'

I had come to believe, even in the short time that I had known Brian, that submerged under all the religion there was a good guy struggling to get out. I thought I saw too the hint of a sense of humour that he was probably afraid to give rein to. The writers of the gospels didn't recount any instances of Jesus having a sense of humour which somehow runs contrary to the belief that he was perfect man. To be perfect he would have had to have a sense of humour to help him cope with all the imperfections and absurdities of being human.

'Do you know,' I said, 'the one thing that I dread about going into this home, if they'll have me?'

'No.'

'It's meeting fellas like you that'd spend their time trying to convert me. If you start it I can ask you to leave and not to come back. In the home I'd be trapped.' The hint of a smile crossed his lips. I wasn't sure whether it was amusement or pity:

'Point taken,' he said, 'but I'll go on praying for you. I'll send in the form and I wish you good luck from the house of Lord.'

'Good man, Brian,' I said, not sure why I said it but I could think of nothing else to say. He left and I never saw him again.

CHAPTER 14

About five weeks after my application went in I received a letter from the Home. It informed me that they would take me, and offered me a place sharing a double room with another man. In due course they would allocate to me a single room when one became available. A bit like the hungry tramp who was offered a regular snack of bread and cheese and if he survived long enough he would qualify for a daily dinner. I didn't fancy sharing with a stranger but if I turned it down I would have to try somewhere else and might have to come back, cap in hand, and agree to share, by which time the place might be taken. Mary brought me to see the room. It was in the old original part of the house and was adequate. I didn't meet the other occupant which was fortunate, as if I had I would almost certainly have turned down the offer. Along the corridor there was a sitting area with television and four or five residents of both sexes sitting on chairs in various stages of decay. There was a smell of urine masked by disinfectant which was familiar to me from having visited parishioners in old peoples' homes over the years. Imagining myself sitting in that half circle on the landing watching television, I was reminded of the psychiatric hospital medical superintendent in a Chekhov short story who ended up in a bed in one of the wards of his own hospital.

I came to the conclusion that I had no option. Mary agreed and encouraged me with the hope that I would not have to wait too long for a single room. She wrote for me and accepted the offer.

Siobhán helped me to collect clothes and some personal things and put them into a suitcase. On the appointed day Mary brought me to the Home and along with a nurse she helped me to settle in. By the time she left I had an emptiness in my head, a fullness in my chest and a vaguely nauseous feeling in the pit of my stomach. The other occupant of the room was nowhere to be seen. I lay on the bed trying to convince myself that I would come to terms with it and I fell deeply asleep. I was wakened by the sound of a colossal belch and sat up to see my roommate sitting on his bed trying to take off his sock.

'Hello, my name's John,' I said. He did not respond and continued to struggle with the half-off sock. He didn't even look in my direction. I said it again. Still no response. I raised my voice and repeated it. He looked towards me, grunted and continued to pull at his sock. Over the years I didn't often blaspheme; it seemed to be a contradiction to what I stood for in those days but:

'Jesus,' I said to myself, 'what have I let myself in for,' and lay back on my side on the bed so that I could keep an eye on my roommate. Eventually he pulled the sock by the toe as far as his reach would allow but the top of it was still above his ankle. He looked puzzled and reached for the sock on the other foot. At this stage I thought he'd fall off the bed. My contorted frame didn't leave me in any position to help, but I thought I ought to say something in the certainty that my roommate would either ignore me or just grunt. At that moment there was a knock on the door and a middle-aged nurse came in.

'Fred you know you're not to take off your socks.' Fred muttered something that I was almost certain was: 'fuck off.' The nurse undaunted pulled up Fred's sock and swivelled him around until he was lying on his bed.

'Have you been introduced?' the nurse asked.

'I introduced myself, but I don't think he heard,' I said. She came over to me held out her hand and said:

'I'm Maria.'

'I'm John.'

'He heard you all right. He's just a little bit odd. You'll get used to him.' Time proved both of these reassurances false: he was nuts and I never became used to him!

Maria gave me a rundown on the routine of the house. In view of my difficulty walking, she confirmed that they would bring my meals on a tray to my room. I was greatly relieved by this; while I didn't want to be standoffish, I didn't relish, in the circumstances, the prospect of making conversation at meals three times a day. It did mean, however, that I spent a good deal of my time in my room and it led to bouts of cabin fever. I was able to relieve this with the help of a nurse who sometimes brought me down the corridor to the sitting area on the landing. The chaplain, who was the local rector, knew my story. I liked him. He dropped in from time to time for a chat and to see if there was anything that he could do for me. Spending so much time in my room did have its upside. Fred, after he went down to breakfast, seldom appeared again until after lunch. He always came back around three o'clock, sat on the side of his bed, discarded his slippers and began to take off his socks. Occasionally he was able to take one off completely but never succeeded in getting both off. He would eventually give up, lie down on his bed and fall asleep. When he woke he would struggle again with his socks and when he had them in such a state that he was able to put his feet into his slippers he was gone again until evening when one of the nurses brought him back and helped him into bed. I shared that room with Fred for the best part of six months and during that time he never spoke one word to me.

Alcohol in rooms was not allowed, but Peter and Tony kept me supplied with a naggin of brandy for medicinal purposes; when I felt absolutely wretched a slug or two was a wonderful pick-me-up. I became convinced, however, that the brandy was disappearing faster than I was using it and that Fred was helping himself while I was asleep. I used a tip that a parishioner had given me years before: I turned the bottle upside down marked the level of the liquid and replaced it right way up in my locker. This ruse confirmed that somebody was helping themselves. I said nothing as Fred probably needed it as badly as I did. As it transpired I wronged the poor devil; a cleaner was summarily dismissed for arriving into work 'under the influence'. She was a decent woman and I felt sorry for her. I felt even sorrier for whoever had to live with her.

One day another resident came to my room and asked me if I would like to join a reading group that met on Tuesday mornings. I was delighted to have been asked and on the next Tuesday one of the nurses came with a wheel-chair and brought me to meet the other three members of the group, two men and a woman. They were all *compos mentis* and interesting people. I looked forward to these meetings and they forced me not to be lazy about my reading. The other group that met was a healer prayer group. I couldn't help but think that in the circumstances they had a job on their hands.

I became used to the routine of the house insofar as I took part in it. Peter and Tony came regularly on Saturday mornings. They always brought some treat or other. Mary came on a weekday evening and Siobhán came quite often too. I sensed that Siobhán was lighter in herself than she had been for a long time. Then on one of her visits out of the blue she said:

'I have a surprise for you: Judy and I are back together. She's moved in and we're very happy.'

'I'm delighted for you. I'm delighted you're happy. You deserve to be,' I said, and I meant it.

I was of course surprised, but on reflection I wasn't. I had been sorry when things hadn't worked out between them. Judy came with Siobhán on her next visit and it was as natural as if they had never separated. I knew that Kate would have been glad that Siobhán was happy and that she and Judy were there for each other.

Kate had always been grateful for all that Judy had done for Siobhán in their early years in Dublin.

After about six months sharing with Fred, a single room became vacant in the new wing and I moved down there. Fred had been in the home much longer than I had so I wasn't sure whether the management believed that he was better not be on his own or that a defunct cleric had precedence over a non-communicative oddity with an obsession with his socks. Whichever it was I was glad to make the move.

The rooms in the new wing were purpose designed for an old people's home. There is a sit-down shower in the small bathroom off the room. I need the help of a nurse or a care assistant to shower, and washing and shaving in the morning are a day's work. Even when I lived with Siobhán I had been determined not to become a smelly old man but now I am slowly losing the battle. The medical expectation that my arthritic pain might burn out has been only partly realised. It has reduced greatly but it hasn't gone. Apart from pain, the passage of time has left me frail and weak. I no longer do the few gentle exercises I used to do to keep a modicum of independent movement. I am dependent on help for almost everything except to think. My mind is still functioning well, although I can't remember names. Nor can I read for long without falling asleep.

On warm days a care assistant wheels me out to sit in the sun in the garden. On these outings I meet other residents, some in wheelchairs and some ambulatory whom I don't know, and some I have never seen before. I, of course, am a complete stranger to them too and wonder if any of them think that I was segregated, except for a brief spell on warm sunny days, because I was an atheist; that pariah caste in religion-obsessed Ireland. I had no doubt that, despite the fact that I know that religious belief was based on fallacies, I know that their religion is a great source of strength and security to many people and I have no right, nor any desire to interfere with that. I have known many former parishioners, good people, to whom it would never have occurred to put their faith under rational scrutiny. The simple faith they had been brought up with meant a great deal to them. It would have been unconscionable of me to interfere with it. I also believe that people like this should respect my right to dissent. There is a caste of proselytising evangelical Protestant, that I seldom encountered, like Brian, but more pushy, that I would, if it arose, be prepared to challenge but I know I would be wasting my time since people like that are impervious to reason.

Time is creeping up on me. I now spend most of my time in bed except for a few hours every day when they lift me out with the help of a hoist and I sit for a while beside my bed in a chair festooned with air cushions and pillows. I can do nothing for myself apart from read my book that the nurse props up on a stand in front of me. Every morning I have to be washed and shaved. The nurses and care assistants are patient and good, but I can see in the eyes of family when they come, something of their pity and pain at my condition. The doctor gives me the impression that my heart is in an advanced stage of failure and might give up at any moment. I wish that it would.

It is clear to me that it is long past time that I was gone. I have served any useful purpose I might have had in this world. I never cease to be grateful that I have always been loved and had someone to love. I have forgotten the particularities of most of my time in the ministry, but occasionally I remember a vignette in which I was able to help to relieve somebody's anxiety or fear. I remember people of every conceivable kind, all trying in their own particular, and often peculiar, way to make some sense of the hand that life had dealt them. I had for long believed that to love, care for and support each other are all we can salvage from living in this mysterious world with its vast preponderance of pain and suffering. Much of this pain and suffering is self-inflicted, depending on how much freewill we think we have, and much of it inflicted upon us by the vagaries of nature.

I have never feared death, but know that I can't be certain that I won't fear it when confronted by it. Now that I am in its vicinity I have no fear and on the contrary I wish for it to come. It would solve a lot of problems for those who care for me, for my family and for myself. I want to die now. I had often thought how I would kill myself if this time came and I found I had had enough. I had always thought that the simplest thing was to walk into the sea, but I'm not even able to walk to the door of my room. There is nothing I can do on my own. I would need help to end it. Who would help me and how? I sometimes think of the Nazi leaders who had little capsules to bite on if they were captured. Where would I find a little capsule? I can't ask anybody. They might be scandalised and if they weren't and were willing to help they might end up in jail.

My life is nothing but a burden to me and to everyone around me, in fact my rapid decline is hellish. All I can do for myself is think and talk. Why can I not decide that as my condition is well-nigh intolerable that I am free to anticipate the inevitable and end it? It's my life. There are fates worse than death and I'm living one.

I have told the doctor that if something develops that will hasten my death, she is not to intervene, and if I become unconscious she is not to resuscitate me. I asked her that as the law does not allow her to end my life for me, was there any law that prevented her from putting me into a coma, rendering me unconscious so that I could wait to die without pain. She smiled her gentle kindly smile and said:

'The Medical Council would have something to say about that.'

Why in these circumstances do people think they have the right to decide for others that they must live on in agony or misery? Of course society cannot allow people to take their own lives willy-nilly, but when the imminent end of a lived life is no more than constant suffering, why, with careful safeguards and controls, can't a body decide they have had enough and have help to end it simply and with dignity? Religion, that's why. It is yet another delusion of religion to believe somehow that pain and suffering are part of the plan of an all-powerful, all-loving, all-merciful God, and that humans must not confound the purposes of God and take it upon themselves to decide whether to live or die. Some religious people believe that suffering is part of God's plan to bring people closer to him and that eternal bliss will be their reward. If this were so the God they believe in is a God of sadism and not of love. If religious people want to believe this kind of thing they are entitled to, but who gave them the right to impose their delusion on other people? Why do some religious people want the State to impose their version of morality on people who don't share their beliefs or their version of morality – contraception, divorce, abortion, Sharia law?

These are religious people who believe they know the mind of God and that people who disagree with them don't have rights in these matters.

They believe in a God that I and millions of other people believe does not exist. I do not know the truth for certain but neither do they.

I told my family of my wish to end my misery. After all we do it for animals, why not for human animals, for that's what we are, animals who happen to have the capacity to make ourselves the object of our own thought, to reflect on these kinds of issue. Siobhán and Peter and Tony sympathise, but I'm not sure if Peter took me seriously:

'On our next visit we'll bring a gun.'

'Well you'll have to pull the trigger,' I replied, 'for I won't be able.'

'And even if you were you'd probably miss.' Peter always gave me something to laugh about.

Siobhán told me on one of her visits that there is no reason in this day and age why anyone should suffer pain:

'No,' I replied, 'they keep physical pain at bay, but it's the emotional and mental pain I suffer and because of the trouble I cause. Even more so it's the indignity of not being able to do anything for myself, of being washed and shaved and having my pad changed.' Tears welled up and ran down my face. Siobhán came over to me, wiped them away and held my head gently in both hands.

'You're doing fine,' she said, 'you're brave; it can't last for ever.' There was a part of Kate that hadn't died.

When I talked to Mary about it she seemed to believe that there was a case to be made for euthanasia for somebody in pain with terminal cancer and a pretty predictable time to live. As pain was kept at bay she didn't think it was justified to end the misery of someone with such an indefinite time to live. I had learned over the years that it made for peace and harmony not to argue with Mary.

The doctor is successful in keeping me largely free of pain. I also have the anaesthesia of sleep. Sometimes I waken from deep, dreamless, pill-induced sleep, and would return to this unconscious sleep akin to death, but cannot. When I waken nothing has changed and I must wait and hope that the time will soon come that I simply won't emerge again into the stark reality of my predicament. One morning when I woke I shocked a new young nurse who was in the room when I said:

'Oh no! I'm not still here.' She told the senior nurse, who knew me well and tried to explain. The fact is that I am not able to end it, so I have no option but to endure it. I have been one of the lucky ones, I've had a good life; the privilege of always having had the necessities of life, I didn't have to go to war and above all I've had the joy of loving and being loved. Most human lives begin with joy, hope and expectation and end in grief, pain or tragedy. As I lie here waiting, waiting, waiting, I believe that life is largely beyond our control. Anything in which I appeared to have had choice I am convinced that I did not, because of the imposition of heredity laid down in the womb, with perhaps some influence from my early environment. When I look back I don't believe that I had freedom to choose the bank, college, marriage to Jennifer, the ministry, leaving the Church, Kate and much more. I believe that as far as all these were concerned they were virtually, if not entirely, determined; I could have done no other for no other reason than that I was not free to, because of factors over which I had no control. In life we are faced constantly with options. We appear to be free to choose but I have grave doubts that we are. I believe that we have little or no choice as to which option we choose.

I listen for the footsteps on the passage outside that slow down and stop at my door. I wait for the handle to turn and despite everything I'm glad when it does, even when it's Katzia the cleaner with nothing more than cheery chat. When it's one of the family or Siobhán it's a joy and I'm glad that there's somebody who cares enough to come.

About the Author

Patrick Semple is a former Church of Ireland clergyman. Patrick has had two volumes of memoirs published, and two collections of poems. He was editor of 'A Parish Adult Education Handbook,' and ghost wrote 'That Could Never Be,' a memoir by Kevin Dalton. He has had short stories published and broadcast. His novel 'Transient Beings' was published in 2012 followed by his travelogue 'Curious Cargo'. In 2013 his creative writing guide 'Being Published' and his collection of short stories 'Slices Of Life' were published. 2014 sees a second collection of short stories 'Another Slice?' and this sequel to his novel 'Transient Beings' being published

Patrick has taught a creative writing course at the National University of Ireland Maynooth, Adult Education Department and does regular readings of his work in Kempten, Bavaria.

He has a website at ***www.patricksemple.ie***

Other Books by Patrick Semple

Transient Beings

A novel

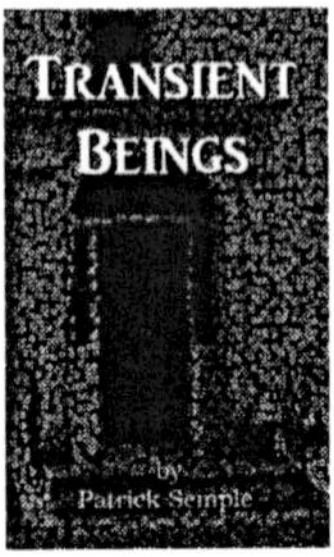

Some transient beings come from the past and pass through the present and some in the present refuse to leave the past. How long will the idyllic rectory in the heart of rural Ireland in the 1970s hide the secrets of those who live behind its walls?

'There is no greater heresy than that the office sanctifies the holder of it.' This is as true for the rector's wife as it is for the rector.

Curious Cargo

A travelogue

This is an account of voyages taken by Patrick and his wife Hilary on cargo vessels carrying everything from bananas to buses. It is the kind of travelling the world thinks has passed into folklore. Midnight coffee on the bridge with the captain; weeks at sea between ports; colour, culture and novelty when you put to shore. There are storms and placid sunlit seas. There is the sound of the ocean and all the while "*the machine is machining*".

Slices of Life

A collection of short stories

These stories are the observations of a person who has spent a lifetime serving other people. Each story tells us something about human nature and the lessons learnt from observing the lives of others. Every story is a slice of life.

Lightning Source UK Ltd.
Milton Keynes UK
UKOW04f1140250714

235754UK00001B/3/P

9 781907 215230